Reveal

A Second Chance Hate To Love Billionaire Romance

Heart of Stone Angela & Brent
Book 3

Chiquita Dennie

304 Publishing Company

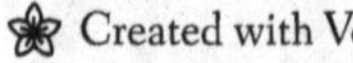 Created with Vellum

This book is dedicated to my family, especially (Rhonda Dennie, Grandma, and Aunt Marcia) for always believing in me. Also, I want to shout out my big Brent Dennie, JD, Christopher, Lil James, Jazzypoo, my sisters, and best friends from Memphis: Nita, San, Reese, Jennifer, LA besties Tavi & Tiffany for always supporting me. Shout out to all of my cousins, nieces, and nephews.

Author Inspiration

"Never allow anyone to steal your joy. It doesn't matter how many times someone says you can't do something. Invest in yourself—even if it's just writing down what your goals and plans are. Starting small can lead to bigger things."

—Chiquita Dennie

Latest Releases from Chiquita Dennie

Pressure(A Driven World Novel)
Until Serena(HEA World Novel)
Exposed (Salvation Society Novel)
Heart of Stone, Book 4 (Jessica and Joseph)
She's All I Need
Something Gaine(Romantic Comedy)
Upcoming Releases (2023/2024):
Something Earned (Romantic Comedy)
The Carrington Cartel
Nicco-TN Seal Security Book 3
Something Borrowed(Romantic Comedy
Knox-TN Seal Security Book 4

Disclaimer

This work of fiction contains strong language and explicit sexual content and is only intended for mature readers. This story may contain unconventional situations, language, and sexual encounters that may offend some readers.I would recommend another book. This book is for mature readers (18+).

Introduction

Are you signed up for my newsletter?

Join today and find out all the latest in new releases, contests, giveaways, sneak peeks and more.

www.chiquitadennie.com

Synopsis

Could an accidental pregnancy be the best thing to ever happen to them?

Brent:

Going to that party was supposed to be fun. I'd catch up with old friends and reminisce a bit.

Instead, I get the surprise of my life.

Angela, my ex-girlfriend, is pregnant.

And the baby is mine.

Angela:

I've always loved Brent.

He was my college sweetheart, my on and off boyfriend for years after that, and finally my hook up one Valentine's Day.

He's also the one who knocked me up.

Now I need to prove to him that I've changed and that I'm ready to settle down.

Brent wanted to marry Angela once, but will he be able to trust her after everything that's happened?

Previously in Heart of Stone
Book 2

Angela

Granny had called me over to help celebrate Jordan's engagement, wedding, and pregnancy announcement. At first, I'd declined because I always avoided being around Brent, but whenever Granny called and cursed me out, then I had to do what she wanted.

My makeup was a little light today, just a little mascara and lip-gloss. I checked out my long, flowy maxi-dress with the side pockets and off-the-shoulder sleeves that hopefully covered any signs of me being pregnant.

As soon as Emery and Jordan found out, they'd pushed me to tell Brent, but I was still nervous about whether he'd be open to the possibility of being a father, now that we'd broken up.

During my years of dating, my goal had always been to not fall in love. After dealing with abandonment issues, I didn't want to put my all into another situation just to be disappointed. Somehow, Brent had torn my walls down and helped me love. Brent thought I kept him at arm's length, but deep inside, I was in love with him.

There was a knock on my car window. "Are you coming inside?" Granny asked, standing at my car door with her hands on her hips.

I grabbed my purse and the present I'd purchased for Jordan and Damon, then unlocked the door. "Old lady, why are you out here?" I sassed. "Did you think I wouldn't show up?" I put my hand on my hip, imitating her posture.

"Girl, your best bet is to get inside, so everybody can start eating before this food gets cold. I have a date tonight, and you're blocking my time."

"Date with who?" I questioned.

"Pops! My husband, of course. Now, what did you bring me?" Granny inquired, peering into my bags.

I followed her into the house and heard loud laughing and talking in the kitchen. I noticed Emery and her parents in the kitchen with JJ. "Hello, family," I greeted them. "What's going on?"

"She finally came out of her cave!" Emery cried. "Granny, did you have to bribe her to get her here?"

"Emery, hush," Granny chastised. "You're the last person who should talk about someone staying away. Let's not talk about your secrets, honey." She picked JJ up off the floor and kissed his forehead.

"Granny, you always take Angela's side," Emery said and rolled her eyes.

"Whatever, Emery," I said. "I'm not staying long, anyway. I have a few appointments, so I have to get back to the salon."

"You might as well get comfortable," Pops joked. "You're staying to eat and hang out." He hugged me as I neared him to head outside to the patio.

"How are you feeling, Pops?" I asked. "Granny told

me you've been doing good, eating better, and taking her out on the town, keeping her young."

"You know, *she* keeps *me* young," he replied. "How are you feeling? I didn't say anything to you about this little bundle of joy you're carrying, but I'm excited for another grandbaby."

Granny passed me a glass of lemonade as I took my phone out of my purse and moved my appointments around for another day. I could tell this would be a lengthy family celebration. "Thanks, Granny," I said. "I'm coming to terms with things, Pops. Who all is here, anyway?" I inquired.

"Jordan's family, Damon's parents, and the usual people," Emery responded. "Brent and a few friends from church."

We all took our drinks and followed Emery's parents to the backyard celebration. Emery had hired the same decorator from Jackson's party last year when he'd signed a new team. They had gold-and-silver balloons hanging around, white linen tablecloths, and a kids' section with games, toys, and a small candy stand.

"Wow, Anthony was invited?" I asked.

"Girl, we've moved on so far from his drama with Teresa," Emery responded. "I told Jordan when we started planning this that I'm fine with him coming around. I've forgiven him, and Jackson has no problems with him—as long as he doesn't get out of line."

"I guess," I replied, "but if that happened to me, I would've cut his dick off and made him sleep with one eye open."

"Your mind is so warped," Emery answered.

I shrugged and picked up a plate to fill it with barbeque, mac and cheese, and Granny's famous potato salad. "Hey, Damon," I greeted him. "Congrats on every-thing." I gave him a one-armed hug as I filled my plate. Jordan walked up behind him and kissed his lips.

"Thanks, Angela," Damon replied. "I appreciate you coming today and celebrating with us. It was a long road to get your girl to see I was for real, and now, we're married and about to have a baby." He hugged Jordan close and rubbed his hand over her pregnant stomach.

I felt the love in the air and looked across the yard at all the couples: Emery's parents; Jordan's parents—hell, even Anthony had someone who'd helped settle him down. I didn't see Brent around. I guess he'd decided to not come.

"He couldn't come because of work," Jordan said, noticing me looking around. "He was closing a big deal today."

Releasing a breath, I turned back around and picked up another glass of lemonade, then sat at the table with Granny, Emery, and Pops. The deejay played music, and some of the kids got up and danced. Damon pulled Jordan into his lap and watched as Tessa tried to follow JJ's steps and floss. We all laughed and cheered her on as I danced in my seat.

"All right, now, little girl," Granny scolded me. "Don't get too hot with that little ass popping in your seat."

Everyone laughed at her, putting me on the spot.

"Granny, I learned my moves from you," I said. "Stop hating. Besides, didn't you get Pops because of your dance moves?" I moved more in my seat as the music played.

Her eyes narrowed in anger, and she flicked me off. Emery snickered next to her. DJ ran over to the table, right as Brent walked toward us. I smelled his cologne as he came near.

"Auntie Angela and Uncle Bee, when is your baby due?" DJ asked, and the entire table went quiet.

Brent laughed at DJ's question and playfully tickled him. "Little man, Angela isn't pregnant," Brent said.

Frozen in place, I looked at Emery and Granny, praying they could help get me out of this situation. Everyone stared back at me, not making any eye contact with Brent.

"Yes, she is, Uncle Bee," DJ said. "I'm going to be a big cousin, right, Mommy?"

Jordan fumbled with her hands, nervous about him blowing my cover. She picked DJ up to take him away from the table.

"The only person who's pregnant next to Emery is Jordan," Brent insisted. "No way a man would get Angela pregnant."

"Excuse me?!" I exploded.

"Angela, come on now," Brent said. "We both know you're not mother material. You've never had the time or focus to be someone's mother."

I stood and rubbed my stomach. I was four months along. I was a thick girl, so you could hardly tell, with me already having a little pouch. I hadn't been with anyone since I found out. I was trying to come to terms with who the father was. I had planned on calling Jeremy next week and letting him know it was a possibility that he could be the father.

Brent stopped laughing, and his face went completely frozen. His eyebrows furrowed, and his hands tightened into fists. The anger across his face was something I didn't want to see because I knew he was hurt and disappointed. "When did you find out?" Brent asked. "Who's the father?"

The lump in my throat grew and caused me to stumble over my answer. Damon and Jackson stood and tried to pull Brent away. Granny continued eating as Pops shook his head.

"We can talk about this later," I replied. "Today is about Jordan and Damon."

Brent shook his head in frustration and walked off.

I decided to follow him to smooth things over. "Brent, please listen to me. I didn't want to tell you like this, okay?" I tried to grip his hand to stop him.

He jerked away from me and headed into the house, where he stopped and turned around, facing me with an angry scowl. "You have to be the most selfish bitch I've ever met!" Brent shouted.

"I understand you're upset, so I'll let your little comment slide, but don't let that word slip out of your mouth again."

Brent waved me off and moved closer to my face, seething. His lips were so beautiful and plump. I shook away my horny thoughts and focused on explaining the situation.

His gaze wandered slowly down my body. "Angela, you need to realize that I'm not running after you anymore. That's why I broke up with you in the first place. You're so selfish and only want things your way. You always forget about my needs."

A cold tremor ran through my body. "What do you want from me?"

"You piss me off!" Every fiber of his body shivered in anger.

"I'm sorry," I whispered.

Emery and Jordan came inside.

Brent looked behind me and shook his head in frustration. "How long did you know?" he questioned them both.

No one answered, and he turned to walk out. I reached out to stop him, but Emery and Jordan stopped me from going after him. I broke down crying in their arms. They gripped me close as Granny came trickling in with a plate of food.

"Calm down, Angela," Emery said. "You can't get stressed. It'll upset the baby." She rubbed my back as Jordan helped comfort me.

"He hates me!" I cried out.

Chapter One

Angela

Two Weeks Later.

I'd just left Jordan and Damon's house, where I was visiting Isabella, and it was quiet inside Sybil's as I sat, waiting for Brent to show up. Thinking back on the day I'd slept with Brent, a flutter ran over my body.

I'd called Brent to talk about what went wrong between us. He'd moved on to Lauren for a little while and became engaged. After a few months, I guess things didn't work out, because around the time Emery and Jackson got married, Brent and Lauren broke up.

"I don't like your attitude when you're like this," I remarked without a trace of humor showing on my face.

"What do you want from me, Angela?" Brent asked. "We both wanted different things, and I moved on. Baby, you can't keep stringing me along." He ran a hand over his face.

"I made a mistake, Brent. You knew what our relationship was and where I came from. Don't make it seem like this was something new. I care for you, but marriage and

kids aren't in my future. Why can't we go back to what we had?" I asked and blinked my tears away.

He closed his eyes and tried to think. "I need time to think about this," he said, holding out his palm.

I decided that it was now or never; if this would be my last chance with Brent, I wanted to feel his body against mine. I straddled his lap. "Baby, please let us have tonight."

"Just tonight." He spoke the words against my skin as a trail of kisses ran up my arm.

All the love I had for this man came back full force as we stared into each other's eyes. Brent had always been the guy who could please me in every way. Lately, I had been spending time with a new friend, Jeremy, and he wasn't bad in the bedroom, but something about Brent bending me over with his long body up against my back, sliding in and out of my pussy, gave me a feeling of home.

I wrapped my arms around his neck and leaned over to kiss his lips, nice and slow. He pulled away, drew in a long breath, and picked me up, then took me to the bedroom. I was glad I'd gotten waxed earlier in the day because it had been a while since we'd been together.

Brent opened the door and laid me on the bed. I helped him out of his shirt and pants. It was rare that he didn't wear a suit. Seeing his jeans, jewelry, and white t-shirt made him even sexier. A man who could go from the boardroom to the streets pulled at my heart.

"Did you get a haircut today?" I questioned, distracted because he didn't get it done by me. Everyone knew that I was the only one who did my friends' or family's hair.

"Is that what you want to discuss right now?" Brent grimaced.

A cocky smirk appeared on my face.

Brent bent, and I met him halfway with a kiss. I gripped his shoulders as our kisses heated up, and our tongues fought to conquer each other.

"I love you, Angela," Brent moaned, squeezing my thigh. His hands skimmed gently over my wide hips and down my silky-smooth legs.

"Make me feel good, baby," I responded, my body aching with longing as I spread my legs, waiting for his lips to touch me.

Afterwards, we didn't talk for a few weeks, and he flew out to California on business. Emery and Jordan kept asking if I wanted more now that I'd gone so long without him in my life. Dating other men allowed me to keep feelings out of the equation because nothing I got from having sex and cocktails every blue moon made me want to call them again. Brent wasn't a social media type of guy, but I knew posting pictures of different places I went to with other men would get back to him. Then, we'd fight and fall back into our old ways. My mistake of thinking I still had a hold on his heart showed up with a photo of some woman and him, shirtless in bed.

I ran a hand across my stomach as the baby kicked, and I smiled. I remembered the day we took the test in Granny's bathroom, and I almost passed out from shock. I had been experiencing weird food cravings like ice cream and pickles. Crying at the drop of a hat, even on little things like someone parking in my parking space at work. I took a test one day and still couldn't believe I was pregnant. I kept fighting it in my head, thinking no one should punish me with a child. Shit, I was still growing up and wanted no responsibilities—besides running my business.

"Wow! Angela Jones, mother-to-be," Emery muttered to herself as I slid down on the bathroom floor, shaking my head in disbelief. Flashing back to the amount of times I had laughed at my friends who became pregnant from a one-night stand and here I was, in the same boat.

"I need a second opinion. Emery, go buy another ten tests. All the warnings say to get a second opinion, and your fertile ass might have put some voodoo on me," I spat, standing and throwing the test in the trashcan.

"Angela, calm down. Stress isn't good for the baby," Emery said, and I glared at her, throwing the middle finger up.

"I'm not pregnant!" I whispered harshly, crossing myself and turning on the water faucet to splash water at Emery for tainting me with her statement.

"Agh, Angela, stop! You're such a dingbat. It's too late for prayers, honey. Welcome to the Mommy Club."

Chapter Two

Angela

"Angela! Angela!" Brent shouted and waved his hand in front of my face.

I must have zoned out. A small shiver ran up my spine as I sat across from the only person who loved me—besides Granny, Jordan, and Emery. I held a finger up for him to wait and drank a sip of water. "Sorry, my throat's a little dry."

He leaned back with one arm resting along the back of the booth. His other hand rested on top of the table, with his eyes piercing through me. I felt a knot in my throat at having to go through this confrontation alone.

"So, when—"

"It was around Valentine's Day. You came to visit, and we caught up, and then this happened." I waved my hand over my stomach, showing off my burgeoning baby bump.

"Are you sure it's mine?"

"Yes, and before you go into bitter baby daddy mode, I tried calling you awhile back, but you blocked me after your little fiancée mishap."

"Mishap? Angela, you have some damn nerve. You tried to fight her in the restaurant when we announced our engagement. Look, I expected more from you, and I guess you proved me right," Brent replied.

"Hi, did you want to order now that your guest has arrived?" the waitress asked and pulled out her notepad and pen.

Brent waved her off, signaling that he wasn't eating anything. This sit-down wasn't going as I had planned.

"Um, I'll just get a salad, fries, and a milkshake."

"Should you be eating all that junk food?" Brent questioned, annoyed at my food choices. I rolled my eyes and passed the menu over to the waitress.

"You never cared about what I ate before," I answered, taking another sip of water.

"You weren't pregnant with my baby before," Brent responded and leaned onto the table with his hands clasped together.

"Oh, so, *now* you're claiming my baby," I said and pursed my lips together.

Brent ran a hand down his face and licked his thick, chocolate-colored lips. He'd grown a beard that lined up nicely with his low-cut, tapered fade. "I'm not your enemy, Angela—"

"I never—"

Brent held a hand up to stop me from talking. "I've known you since middle school, through high school, and damn-near proposed to you after college. I get it; you've never wanted to be that person. You may have seen it as me trying to make you into something you're not—but baby, all I wanted was to love you."

"I know that, Brent."

"All we have between us is this baby, and I will be the best father to our child. But going forward, I don't want to have anything to do with you if it doesn't pertain to the kid," Brent said and stood, taking his wallet out and leaving forty dollars on the table for a meal he didn't order.

"Brent, wait!" I yelled.

I hadn't expected him to walk out on me like he just did, but with our lack of communication over the past few months, and him working out in California, I guess I shouldn't have been surprised. I felt as if our connection had been broken beyond repair.

Hearing my phone buzz, I ignored the message from my maternal grandmother.

Mildred's Mom: *Hi, Angela. I was thinking about you and wanted to see if we could meet and talk.*

She hadn't wanted to talk to me in the last twenty or so years I'd been living in the same city as her. Ever since my mom and dad broke up, and then she went on a drinking binge and lost her ability to care for me, it seemed like that part of the family didn't want to have anything to do with me, like I was cursed and destined to bring more bad luck on them or something.

Suddenly, my phone rang, and Emery's name flashed across it. "How did it go?" she asked quietly.

"Like I expected it to go. He hates me for keeping the pregnancy a secret. I knew this would happen at some point, but I honestly didn't know who the father was, and you know my family dynamics. It was a struggle for me to even decide to raise a child with my fucked-up background and parents. It wasn't like I had a positive role model from either parent."

"Don't beat yourself up. Brent just needs some time,

and I'll have Jackson talk with him to see where his head is at."

"I don't know if that's a good idea, Emery. He's pissed that everyone knew except him. I doubt adding Jackson into the fold would help matters any."

I sighed through the phone and mentally debated on what my life would look like once I had this child. I burst out into laughter as Emery continued talking.

"Angela! Angela! What's so damn funny? You were just sad and about to cry over Brent." Hormones had me snapping at people, and sometimes if they looked at me wrong, I'd burst into tears from fear they'd yell at me.

"Oh, my God! I just realized I'm going to be somebody's mother."

The laughter helped keep the tears at bay because Brent would probably never forgive me for keeping the secret for so long. Even if it weren't a plan, he'd see that our mutual families and friends knew before him and could have gotten in touch with him at any point. Our arguments and clashes often went on for months, resulting in us not talking to each other.

My pregnancy wasn't the best timing in the world, so wallowing in pity every night and debating if he was the father was another issue I didn't want everyone to know about. As my single friends went out on dates, I stayed home, thinking about my future as a single woman and how I would manage things. The days of Angela being selfish had to come to an end.

Chapter Three

Brent

Two *Months Later*

I ran and jumped into the passenger side of Jackson's car. I was too nervous to drive and was practically shaking. We'd all gotten the call that Angela was in labor while we were out playing basketball.

"Man, I honestly never saw Angela as a mother," Jackson said, bringing me out of my thoughts.

"Shit, neither did I, man," I replied, placing my phone on vibrate when all of a sudden, I saw an incoming text. Elena, my latest girlfriend, was checking to see about grabbing lunch together.

Elena: *Hey, are you still with the guys?*

Me: *Heading to the hospital.*

Elena: *Angela's having the baby?*

Me: *I believe she is, babe.*

Elena: *Did you want me to come?*

"Elena's texting about wanting to come up to the hospital."

"Has the family met her?"

I blew out a frustrated breath. The only people who had met Elena were my boys Jackson and Damon, and my family.

"Brent, please tell me you've introduced her to Angela?" Jackson asked, weaving in and out of traffic.

Elena: *Brent, hello?*

Me: *I don't think this is the right time.*

"Listen, Angela only needs to worry about bringing our baby into the world safely. I don't want her stressed out right now."

We pulled up to the hospital, and Emery texted the room number that she was in. We hadn't seen each other in person since the diner. I'd texted to check up on the baby, and she'd respond to say the baby was fine. Granny wanted us to get back together, but that ship had sailed.

I pressed the button to silence my phone as we entered the hospital and ran to the labor and delivery ward on the third floor. Angela had gone into labor early, before the girls could surprise her with a shower, or so Jackson told me. They wanted to do it up big. Angela grew up without her parents around, so I knew I needed to be sensitive to her needs and keep my attitude in check.

After getting my badge and putting on the scrubs and facemask, I walked into the room to the sound of loud screaming.

"Oh, my God! Get this thing out of me!" Angela screamed and cried as Emery stood on her left side, running a cool rag over her forehead. Jordan stood on her right side, feeding her ice chips, both of them holding her hand. Granny and Pops stood when I approached and walked toward me.

Pops shook my hand and patted me on the back, smirking. "Good luck with that one, son. There's going to be another one like Angela soon. Get your wallets ready," Pops chortled.

Granny nudged him out of the way as Angela leaned back in the hospital bed, squirming as the doctors and nurses came into the room. "Don't listen to him, baby. You know how Angela can get," Granny said and shook her head as Angela frowned at me.

"You did this to me, asshole. Doctor, I don't want him in here." Angela pointed at me, trying to sit up and take her legs out of the stirrups. Her hair was all plastered over her head, and sweat poured down her face, mixing with tears. At the same time, she was the most beautiful I'd ever seen her.

The doctor and nurse stood frozen, not knowing what to do. Emery grabbed her shoulder to help her lie back down. Granny walked over to her and whispered in her ear. I turned to introduce myself to the doctor as Angela nodded—I assumed that meant she wanted me to stay.

"You must be the father? I'm Dr. Wilson, Leonard Wilson," the doctor told me as he shook my hand, walked over to Angela, and pulled her gown up over her legs, readjusting her to move down further.

"Brent, I'm sorry. Please, don't go," Angela whimpered and reached out for me to come closer. Taking her hand, I kissed her palm and her forehead. The nurse checked her vitals, and as the doctor pressed on her lower abdomen, she squirmed from a contraction.

"All right, Angela, you're ten centimeters dilated. Are you ready to meet your little one?" Dr. Wilson announced as Jordan and Emery high-fived each other, and Angela waved them off.

"I swear if I make it through this, I'm never having

kids again," Angela mumbled, as she leaned up, getting ready to push.

"You got this, bestie," Jordan, along with Emery, cheerfully said at the same time. I felt my phone vibrate in my pocket.

"Whose phone is that?" Angela asked stridently.

"Okay, Angela, I need you to give me a push on the count of three, okay? One... two... three... Now push."

"Agghhh! Please! I can't do this," Angela yelled and fell back on the bed, closing her eyes and breathing hard. I looked into her eyes, knowing the toll it took on her to bring our child into the world.

My phone vibrated again, and I took it out of my pocket to turn it off. Angela snatched it out of my hand.

"Who the fuck... ugh... is Elena?" Angela screamed, eyebrows furrowed, glaring with clenched teeth and following Emery as she coached her in breathing.

I wanted to kiss her lips and let her know she looked beautiful, but I figured with everyone around, she'd probably push me away. I came around to watch as the nurse and doctor worked to guide my baby into the world safely. Emery continued easing Angela's mind, telling her things would be all right, and she had all of us there to help.

"Angela, you need anything?" I asked. "I know women like to have a baby setup, with a bag of clothes for when they're ready to come home. I can have my assistant pick some things up."

"No."

I sighed at her dismissing my question. It was partly my fault after walking out on her a couple months back, when we met at the restaurant to discuss the pregnancy. My entire family texted afterward and wanted to know what was going on, since Granny spilled the beans about us having a kid together.

"Angela, relax and focus; you and Brent are on the same team. Stop pushing him away and let him help you," Jordan said and peered over at me as Angela and I locked eyes.

She started to smile, and I smirked. Suddenly, my phone went off again, and a hard glare dropped across her face like a curtain.

Emery and Jordan both shook their heads in disappointment.

Chapter Four

Angela

I'm over here about to shove a fucking watermelon-sized bigheaded child of yours out of my va jay jay, and you have the nerve to be texting some tramp that probably can't suck your dick the way I used to, I thought snarkily and threw his phone across the room. "Ugh! I hate you so much, Brent," I sniveled and pushed again as the doctor instructed.

Brent tried rubbing my shoulders to comfort me. "You're worried about the wrong thing, baby," Brent responded.

As my tears trickled down my cheeks, Emery tried to wipe them away, and I snatched the napkins out of her hand. This entire pregnancy had me snapping at the people I loved more than usual. Now that I knew Brent was seeing someone, and there was no hope for us getting back together, I needed to just focus on co-parenting from here on out and allow momma bear to take care of herself.

I wanted to dropkick him *and* her, but Granny made me promise to be nice. Ever since he walked out of the restaurant, we hadn't seen each other—besides texting back and forth. I knew I had no right to be mad, seeing as I was the one who didn't want to get married and have kids in the first place, but still my heart hurt.

Before snatching my arm away from his tight grip, I felt a heavy pressure down below, and I winced in pain. Either the baby was coming, or I had to shit—and I'd heard about women not being able to control their bowels during childbirth.

"I see the head, Angela. Give me one good push," Dr. Wilson said excitedly as the nurse stood beside me, ready with a blanket and towels.

"Ugh! Shit! I can feel the baby moving!" I yelled, yanking Brent's shirt and clenching my teeth.

"It's a girl!" the doctor shouted and held her up so I could see her face. I felt exhausted. She was the spitting image of Brent with wild, curly, black hair, small button nose, and dark-chocolate skin tone. Brent released my hand, cut the umbilical cord, and watched as they moved her over to the heat lamp and cleaned her up. Emery and Jordan followed as I felt another tight pressure below.

"Mmm, Dr. Wils..." I muttered.

"Wow! I didn't see this in the sonogram," Dr. Wilson said.

Emery, Jordan, and Brent ran back over to my bedside as I leaned up on my elbows, about to curse him out if something was wrong.

"What is it?" I asked, perplexed by his sudden silence.

"Uhh, Angela, we have another baby coming. I need you to stay calm and push for me."

"What!" we all shouted at the same time.

"You can't be serious! I can only deal with one of them; I didn't order two! What do you mean 'another baby?!' I'm suing this entire fucking hospital! Get me another doctor right now, Emery!" I screamed as another contraction felt like it would split me in two.

Brent walked over to stand behind the doctor, and I tried—with no help from Emery and Jordan—to kick the doctor in the face for not seeing that I was pregnant with twins sooner.

"Brent, I swear to God, when I get out of this, I'm pressing charges on you. I can't believe I'm pregnant with twins. Wait a minute... who in your family has twins?" I pried my eyes open and glared at him as he shrugged and smiled at seeing another baby girl being pulled out of my precious vagina. "I probably should have gone to church more often when Granny asked, because the spawn of Satan has impregnated me with twins," I mumbled, and the doctors and nurses laughed at my pain.

"Remember, on my dad's side, his mom is a twin," Brent said completely nonchalant like this was something that happened every day, like finding an extra twenty dollars in a jeans pocket.

I burst into tears, knowing I would be taking two babies home with me. My entire life had changed in the blink of an eye. Brent threaded a hand through my hair, and I reeled back, pissed that he had the nerve to touch me again.

"Get away from me with your demon dick," I screeched, folding my arms. He chortled and shook his head. "Brent, I don't see this situation as a laughing matter!" I explained haughtily, wiping my nose with my gown. My entire appearance was a mess from realizing I was having twins, Brent dating some new girl, and my grandmother trying to get back in touch with me.

"Princess, stop stressing around my daughters. They feed off your energy, and if they see you crying, *they'll* start crying," Brent responded, grabbing baby one out of Emery's arms to pass her to me.

Gathering my composure, I nodded. "Oh, God, she looks just like you. I'm never having sex again."

"Girl, please. As soon as you're healed up, you'll be ready for another." Brent chuckled and lay in the opposite bed with his shirt off for skin-to-skin contact with our daughters. I rolled my eyes at his statement. "I like Jazmine and Margaret," Brent said.

"Like Margaret Thatcher or something? My child's not going through school with a name of a British prime minister. What about Jazmine and Marcia after Granny's sister?" I said.

He nodded, and we agreed on the names, since we both won in the end.

"You two look so cute. Smile for the camera, Mama," Emery asked.

"Emery, I look a mess. Wait until I put some makeup on to take photos."

"You look beautiful to me, princess," Brent said, and my heart rate kicked up a notch. All the nurses cooed in joy at his admission. Emery just shook her head and continued taking pictures.

"When will they be able to go home?" Brent inquired as the nurse helped me breastfeed Jazmine.

"In a day or two, if everyone is fine, I'll speak with Dr. Wilson and see what he says," Nurse Anderson said, checking my vitals, then Jazmine's.

I figured that I needed to set up a schedule and rework my salon clients. Brent would have to change his schedule and cut down on traveling, as well, so I wouldn't lose business.

"Get out of your head, Angela. I'm proud of you,

princess," Brent said, massaging the back of my neck and kissing my cheek. Closing my eyes, I felt a rush of butterflies in my stomach. Marcia stirred in his arms, He gradually got up and put her back in the crib, then walked over and lifted Jazmine out of my arms to burp her and put her down to sleep.

* * *

"Emery, can you see about getting me some real food please? I can't take this hospital food for one more day.

Brent watched as Nurse Anderson gathered the birth certificates of the girls and had him sign and then passed it over to me. Seeing the names Jazmine Desiree Townsend and Marcia Lynn Townsend alongside Brent Townsend as father, and Angela Jones as mother, I blew a breath out as Brent took my hand, keeping my anxiety at bay. The rejection—and seeing other kids who had a family with both parents—brought on the anxiety and abandonment issues. So, once I grew older, I focused on myself and found solace in the arms of men and the attention they gave me. It inspired me to never give my heart to a man—let alone become a mother—but the moment Brent Townsend walked into class, sweat formed on my forehead, and my hands became clammy. He let me down in front of the whole class when I flirted. He would be the only person who could break my heart if I let him. So, I focused all my energy on not letting anyone get close except my family.

"Sure, Angela. I'll tell Granny and Pops to go home, and we'll get your house together. Jordan can handle rescheduling your clients," Emery suggested, grabbing her purse and hugging Brent, then me, as she walked out of my room with Jordan following.

"You don't need to stay. More than likely, they'll sleep for the rest of the night. I'll call you tomorrow when they wake up."

"I'm fine right where I'm at, sweetheart," Brent answered and leaned back on the couch, briefly closing his eyes.

"I hate when you call me 'sweetheart,'" I stated just to annoy him.

His tall, sexy frame in basketball shorts showcased his dick outline that I loved so much. Shaking off any thoughts of ever having sex again, I adjusted myself in the bed and tensed as I moved wrong. I felt exhausted, hungry, and sore from the stitches. I turned the TV on and covered my body with the blanket as I moved a hand across my stomach that had once held two human beings inside and was now empty. Looking over at Brent as he drifted off to sleep, I felt comforted in knowing I now had my own version of a family.

Chapter Five

Brent

The next day, Angela felt like she looked ugly, sitting in bed, wearing an unflattering hospital gown, hair all over her face, with extra pregnancy weight, and a little splatter of milk on her gown. To me, she'd never looked more beautiful since the first day I met her, when she tried to push up on me in front of everybody. I'd peered at her, fumbling with her hands, and I saw the lump get caught in her throat when I closed the distance between us and tilted her chin, not letting her vulnerability hide what she wanted but couldn't express.

"I'm staying tonight—and *every* night—until all my girls come home. Usually, it takes a few days before you get released," I said.

Angela nodded and pointed at the couch and pillow that the nurse had left for me the night the girls were born.

"That won't work," I said, kicking off my shoes, turning my phone off, lifting the covers and climbing in the bed securing her in my arms with her back to my chest."

"You're not slick, Brent. Your little girlfriend won't like this."

"Elena's the last thing you need to worry about after you just gave birth to two of our kids. I'm so proud of you, princess. I think I'll need to get security though. Dealing with one little girl is bad, let alone two and their crazy momma," I joked, and she bumped into my dick with her butt. Tightening my hold, I lightly bit her ear and rubbed her stomach gently.

She tried to push my hand away from her stomach.

"Stop moving my hand. You were amazing and if you don't stop wiggling around in this bed, you'll end up pregnant again."

"I think you might have me mistaken with your girlfriend."

"Go to sleep, princess."

The next day I helped Angela bring the girls home. At first, I wanted her to come to my place, but she blocked me at every turn. Granny had to talk some sense into her, so she would let me at least drive her home and help get the girls settled. Everyone was there with us, and the kids were running around, excited, waiting to see the new additions to the family. Jordan helped Angela sit on the couch; Jackson brought in Jazmine, and I carried Marcia. Granny already had food cooking, and Pops sat in the chair, watching the kids run in a circle, playing tag. Emery walked by and headed into the kitchen to help Granny get dinner together. The girls had checked out fine and didn't have any complications, so the doctor discharged them. The office knew I'd be taking a few days off to help manage things in my personal life. Taking tips from Emery and Jordan's pregnancies, I would take as much of the burden from Angela as possible, so she could take some time off and enjoy motherhood and not have to worry about working.

"Princess, you need anything?" I asked, staring into her eyes as she pulled Jazmine out of her car seat, wearing the pink outfit that Granny and Pops had bought that read, "I Love My Grandparents."

Emery placed Marcia in her other arm, and Angela shook her head stubbornly. "We're fine, Brent. You can go back to your life now. I'll have my lawyers call you about a visitation schedule that works for us both."

I jerked back at her dismissive tone, darting my eyes between our daughters. Pops started to say something, and I raised my hand. The tension could be cut with a knife. She boldly met my eyes as I knelt right in front of her, holding our kids.

Angela couldn't get rid of me so easily now that we had two kids who depended on both of us to work as a team. "Did that make you feel better?" I questioned.

After a long pause, during which she fought for self-control, she demanded with her cold eyes for me to back down. I wouldn't because I knew she wanted me to stay and fight for us. This time, I would need her to fight for my heart just as much.

"Angela, are you causing problems out here?" Granny demanded, walking into the living room, wiping her hands on a dishtowel.

"Granny, she's fine; nothing I can't handle," I said just as my phone rang. She stiffened, challenging me to answer the call. I knew it was probably Elena because I hadn't called her back in three days.

"Babe, did you take your medicine today?" Jackson came out of the kitchen with JJ following, eating a popsicle. He sat next to Emery on the edge of the couch with an arm around her shoulder, a little cocky smirk plastered on her face.

She kissed him on the lips. "Of course, baby. JJ, who gave you that popsicle before dinner?" Emery teased and pulled him close to her lap.

"He's fine Emery. A little bit won't upset his appetite," Granny said as she found a seat.

Emery agreed and let JJ go, and he sat on the floor next to DJ and Tessa. Damon walked inside talking on the phone, looking frustrated. "What's up, bro?" I asked and dapped him up, giving him a one-shoulder hug.

"Man, these clients are driving me crazy. Plus, my baby momma is dating some new guy and taking off all the time, traveling like she doesn't have a daughter who needs her here at home," Damon replied, helping Jordan out of her seat and placing her on his lap.

"Did you tell Bridget to call Tessa tonight? You know, she missed her scheduled call for the third time yesterday," Jordan said, running a hand over his head. He rubbed up and down her thigh, staring at DJ and Tessa on the floor, watching *The Lion King* for the twentieth time.

With a groan, Damon shifted his eyes up to the ceiling, his expression stilled and grew serious. The second he got married to Jordan and got her pregnant, Bridget seemed to be okay with them being together.

"That girl will never act right. I'm glad you have full custody of Tessa. If I had to deal with her about seeing my grandbaby, it wouldn't turn out good for anybody," Granny spat, standing and heading back into the kitchen.

"Believe me, I don't regret my daughter, but her

mother is another thing altogether. I'm tired, babe. Can we head out? I need a break," Damon said, nuzzling Jordan's neck.

Jordan giggled and blushed. She looked at him in amusement. "Let's have dinner first, and then we can go home."

My phone rang again, and I saw a message from Elena, wanting to meet for dinner.

Elena: *Babe?*

Me: *I can't talk right now.*

Elena: *When can I see you?*

Me: *I'll call you. Angela needs me.*

Elena: *What about what I need?*

Shaking my head at her childish comment. I replied and turned my phone on vibrate. Catching Angela's raised eyes, she rose without haste, looking somber and lost, heading off into the kitchen with Granny.

"Bro, are you staying here with Angela or going home?" Jackson asked.

"For the first few days, I'll kick it here with her to get her used to the girls. But Granny said she would help and stay in the guestroom," I said, following him into the kitchen as everyone gathered around the table to eat. I'd paid for the kitchen to be redone a few years ago as a birthday surprise. The walls were covered in rich cream-and-gold wallpaper that looked like shimmering marble, accompanied by a high, open ceiling, French doors, and a custom Italian marble table that could seat twenty.

I helped Tessa sit in her chair, and DJ followed, climbing into his chair without any help.

"Granny and Pops are staying here. Brent is going

home tonight. I have enough help," Angela stated, having overheard his question.

"I doubt he's the help, Angela, as both of them look just like him in the face," Granny spat, pointing a finger in her face, scolding her for being rude. Her voice rang aloud, like a church bell announcing the second coming. She spun around hard on me, like a top that had lost its center and sat at the end of the table, slumped in her chair.

I wanted to laugh at her attitude, but then it would have given her the attention she craved from me. I refused to go back and forth with her when she was the one who could have avoided this entire situation if she had been honest in the first place.

I ran a hand over my beard and sighed. *She won't make this easy,* I thought. I walked around to the other side of the table to sit between Emery and Jackson. That way I could see Jazmine, and Marcia lying in the crib.

"Don't worry about it, Granny. I'll head home after dinner and call my lawyer tomorrow. I'm not about to fight with Princess while she's up in her feelings," I stated, releasing a harsh breath.

"I guess he told you, huh?" Granny chortled and passed the meatloaf around the table. Angela lowered her head in embarrassment as everybody started talking and joking at the dinner table.

* * *

As much as I didn't want to leave, I needed a break from Angela's attitude and to get my mind right over the situation. I came into the office early, checked my messages, and Elena was blowing me up. I turned the computer on in the office—even though I wanted to take some time off from work.

Barbara, my secretary, came inside, holding a coffee cup and a muffin. "How does it feel to now be a father of twins?" Barbara asked blissfully happy, fully alive with warmth and joy, knowing two more babies would be running around the office. She was at the grandmother age and didn't get to see her grandkids much because they lived out of state. When I told her about my kids, her whole face glowed with excitement.

"Honestly, I feel the same, just have more priorities now. Maybe I need to get a shotgun because I'm not letting them date until they turn fifty," I answered, taking a sip of the coffee.

Barbara laughed at my statement and sat in the chair in front of my desk. Taking the notepad off my desk and pen to run down my schedule for the day, I let out a long, audible breath.

"Brent, give her a little time. Angela's been a new mother for less than a few days, after being a single woman for years. From what I gather, her expectation for her life was simply her career. So, this is a new thing for her—on top of not having her parents in her life," Barbara replied.

"How did you know about her parents?" I questioned, while replying to emails.

"Angela's a tough cookie, and often, when she stops by to meet Emery or you for lunch, we'll talk in the employee lounge. She's tough on the outside and soft on the inside."

"I hear you. For now, I'm going to focus on my kids and my work. The last thing either of us needs is a relationship."

"Did she get the gifts I sent over through Emery?"

"She did and thank you."

"What did you name them?"

"Jazmine and Marcia Townsend."

After returning an email, I looked over at my phone, vibrating on my desk. Elena's name flashed across the screen. I hadn't talked to her since the birth of my babies and dealing with Angela's up-and-down moods wasn't helping. I picked it up and turned it off to get my thoughts together.

"Are they keeping you guys up at night? I know when my niece had her twins, she couldn't sleep for the first two months because one or both would be up crying," Barbara said.

"I'm not sure, Barbara. They stay with Angela full time, and we haven't set a schedule of visitation since they've been home."

"Oh."

"What?"

"Nothing."

"That 'oh' and 'nothing' definitely mean something. What's on your mind?"

"Are you planning on moving in together?"

"Angela and I can't even agree on what the weather is like, so I highly doubt we'd move in together, even though I tried to stay with her when she was released from the hospital. Instead, she refused my help and only wanted Emery and Granny," I said, shrugging my shoulders dismissively.

"After childbirth, a woman's hormones are all over the place. Give her a little time, and she'll come around. Giving her space would help because obviously, she has feelings for you and is trying to fight them."

"Angela having feelings for me is the last thing on my mind. I have enough problems with women. She was the one who hid her pregnancy from me. Now, she's trying to get mad because I started dating someone when I lived in California," I answered, frustrated. When I met her that day at the café, I wanted to curse her out and kiss her all over her face. She was so beautiful and glowing with my babies inside her stomach. At the same time, I couldn't understand how the one person I trusted more than anything in this world would keep such a big secret from me.

My mind drifted back to the time I saw her sitting alone in the student lounge, upset and crying after her mother once again rejected her. I was hanging with my friends, about to go out for the night. Seeing her upset caused me to pause and comfort her, but it wasn't like we were dating at the time. But our friendship did flourish since we hung around the same group of people.

"How long are you going to hold a grudge?"

Annoyed with the conversation, I changed the subject. "Did we receive the contracts from that new account Emery was dealing with? Damon's agency was supposed to sign a deal with a drink company and wanted a new marketing strategy."

"Changing the subject, I see." Barbara chuckled and stood, walking out to her desk, and then came back inside with a file folder. "Don't run from what you two can have, Brent. Now, let me go out here and make these calls. Anything special for lunch today?"

"The usual—a sandwich from the corner bakery is fine."

Barbara nodded and walked out, closing my door softly behind her. I looked through the contract and returned some emails until lunchtime. I wanted to get an update from Angela about how my babies were doing. I started to text her, then decided to put my phone down, distract myself from the bullshit, and give her space. I needed a little time with my friends tonight and some adult conversation.

Chapter Six

Angela

One month after giving birth, I wasn't feeling the extra weight at all and decided to get healthy again. All the women in my circle told me to take it easy, but I wasn't used to this. On top of not being able to just get up and go, I also had to get used to putting my girls' schedule ahead of mine.

"Ugh, I swear, having kids is draining, and not being able to drink is another problem." I scowled at the skinny bitch in front of me on the treadmill as I dragged Emery and Jordan along to work out with me.

"Are you serious, Angela?" Emery asked. "You've only been a mom for a month, and you're already complaining?"

"Yep," I spat sarcastically and wiped my sweat from my brow with the back of my hand. I was breathing heavily, trying to keep up the pace with the girl in front of me.

"What's going on with you? Brent's been helping with the feedings and changing diapers, right?" Emery questioned, taking a sip of her water bottle.

"He has, and we've stayed in contact on a set schedule

because he got it in his head I'd run off with the girls if we didn't have a schedule, you know, since I'm not the committed type or some bullshit. I honestly don't think he would have said something unless someone put the idea in his head." *Maybe it was that bitch he's been dating.*

"Wait, is he talking about a custody hearing?" Emery said, suddenly stopping her machine and turning toward me.

"I don't think so, but if I need to get a lawyer, I'll let you know. Deep down, I know he's pissed still over me keeping things a secret. Then I wouldn't let him help once I came home from the hospital. His little feelings are hurt."

"Honestly, if I were Brent, I'd take you to court," Jordan said, not missing a beat on the treadmill.

My mouth hung agape at her statement. "Whose side are you on, anyway? A few months back, weren't you dealing with your own insecurities and issues with Damon and Bridget, Miss Thing?" I responded, rolling my eyes, pissed that she'd tried to come at me in public. Yeah, I wasn't the motherly type of person, and I did my dirt in the past, but give me a break! These past few months have shown me that having the same mindset of a single woman and partying like I did in college wouldn't hold up today with my responsibilities.

"Look, Angela, don't bring my business into this because you can't be honest with him—*and* yourself. There's been countless times I told you how selfish you were being, hiding from Brent. Now that he's moved on, you want to sit and pout like a baby. Girl, grow up and leave my marriage out of your misplaced feelings," Jordan answered, irritated.

I was almost tempted to get off the treadmill and slap

her across the face, but if your best friends can't tell you the truth, then there's no point having a support system. "Whatever," I said with tightened lips.

"Don't 'whatever' me. That's the problem; everybody lets you get away with stuff and spoils you to spare your feelings. I'm telling you now; things can go right or wrong if you don't change your attitude," Jordan fussed, raising her voice.

"Somebody finally caught a backbone. Damon must have pissed you off or something?"

I watched as she glowered at me and then stormed off. Running behind people was the last thing on my agenda, and I turned the machine up and continued running.

"That wasn't cool, Angela," Emery hissed and walked off to find Jordan.

It was midday, and relaxing with my friends was the top priority, but if I continued on this path and didn't apologize, I'd end up with no friends—on top of no man and family. What I didn't tell the girls was that Brent had done nothing but be sweet and patient with me and the twins. He came over after work and played with the girls, while I stayed in my room, hesitant to interrupt his bonding time with them. I doubt that if we slept together, it would help our situation; it would probably make things even more complicated. The day he came to my house when I came home from the hospital, I knew I was jealous of him moving on. My defense was to push him away before I got hurt by falling back in love with him. Seeing the smiles on my babies' faces, and how protective he was with them, made me want that same attention. I stepped off the treadmill and wiped it down, taking a big gulp of water and walking over to Emery, who was talking with Jordan next to the weights. I nudged her gently on the shoulder and mouthed: *Sorry*. She smiled and wrapped her arm around my shoulder.

"Hold up, girl. You smell. Hit the showers first before you try to hug me. I'm not Damon; I don't need to love you when you're ripe." I chuckled, and she shoved me away and took a quick sniff under her arms and laughed.

"How about we do lunch on you, Angela, to make up for your bullshit."

I threw my hands on my hips, cocked my head to the side with my lips poked out. "Excuse me, did I not just apologize? The friendship handbook that I read didn't state I needed to spend money on you unless it was a holiday, birthday, or anniversary."

"The friendship handbook only exists in your mind when you want something and need to get spoiled by everyone around you. The two of us know you better than anyone, and becoming a mom won't stop us from calling you out on your bullshit when you're wrong. So, yes, you will treat us to lunch—and the most expensive one, at that, since your baby daddy is rich," Emery declared as she dropped the weights onto the machine and gathered her towel up.

I waved off her words and followed as we headed off toward the lockers to take a shower and eat.

* * *

They chose the most expensive place on my credit card. A new Mediterranean place next to the Tiffany Renee Salon that we often visited.

"Are you getting used to breastfeeding? I know when I had DJ, it took me a while to get him to latch on?" Jordan confessed, biting into her falafel sandwich.

We sat on the patio in the shade. It wasn't too busy this time of day, and since Brent was with my girls, I had time to relax and didn't have to rush home.

"The first day, I didn't have a problem with them breastfeeding at the hospital, but after a few days at home, I wasn't feeling equipped to handle the pain. They don't tell you how painful it can be, even when I took maternity classes. Teachers talked about it somewhat, but not fully. Finally, I'm starting to get into a routine, even though I'm tired a lot more and barely go out, a month after becoming a mommy."

"After JJ, I stopped breastfeeding and transitioned him over to a bottle. Don't beat yourself up about what you think you're supposed to do. Every mother is differ-ent, and you'll never live up to some fantasy of the perfect mother. As long as you and Brent love them and raise them in a loving and positive environment, they'll be all right. Besides, you know if you don't, Granny will kick your ass."

"Thanks for the vote of confidence, Emery," I mumbled under my breath.

Taking a bite of a cherry tomato, I poked around at the lettuce, dreading over ordering just a salad and water. I was starving and wanted real food, but the only way I figured I could get back into the same shape I was pre-pregnancy was to stick to better eating habits.

"Is that all you're going to have, Angela?" Emery asked, slicing a piece of her chicken marsala and staring at me playing with my food.

"I had a big breakfast. I'm just not that hungry."

"Please don't get into that headspace about your weight."

"For real, Angela, you're the most confident person I

know. The weight will come off in time. Don't rush and starve yourself."

"Is this about Brent's girlfriend, that model?" Emery questioned.

I shook my head as she narrowed her eyes at me. "I'm not starving myself, and this isn't about Brent. For me to get back comfortable in my own skin and in the right headspace, I decided I want to lose a few pounds. It has nothing to do with a man. Anyway, I wanted to talk to you guys about something."

Before I could speak, my phone rang. It was my assistant was calling from the salon.

Chapter Seven

Angela

"Hey, Kimberly. What's going on?" I asked.

"Hi, Angela. Sorry to bother you while you're on maternity leave. Some girl came up here looking for you," Kimberly said in a rushed whisper.

"What girl, and what did she want?" I asked, shuffling in my seat nervous it had something to do with Brent and his bitch of a girlfriend.

"She said she's your cousin and wanted to talk. I told her I'd relay the message, and when you're back in the salon, you'd call her," Kimberly explained.

"Oh. Thanks, Kim. The next time she comes by, tell her I'm not interested."

"Huh!"

"I don't need any more surprises in my life. My mom and dad's family turned their backs on me a long time ago. I'm good with the family I got with Emery and Jordan," I confessed, winking at them as they looked confused by my side of the conversation.

"Okay, are you coming in this week at all?"

"Possibly. I need to look at my schedule and get back

to you. Tell everyone I miss them, and I'll bring the girls by soon," I said, hanging up the phone.

"What was that about?" Jordan asked.

"Same old thing as usual, long-lost relatives trying to get back into your good graces now that they see you doing well."

"Sounded like Kimberly at the salon. Did you decide when you're going back to work?" Jordan inquired.

"Sometime this week or next. I need to talk with Brent and Granny first and make a schedule that works for everyone. I already had a small area installed for my girls and the other stylists who need to bring their kids if they don't have a babysitter. You guys know my goal is to open more salons, and sitting at home is not what I dreamed for my life. Before I had my girls, I wanted to travel and do hair for high-profile celebrities on top of running my salon."

"I know you talked about that in college all the time. Well, hit Brent up and let him know if you can't get him to watch the girls, or if Granny can't, I can help out," Jordan said.

"Thanks, ladies. Let's conquer one thing at a time. So, catch me up on what you've been doing before I head home to my babies."

We talked, laughed, and joked around for the next few hours before finally parting ways. I pulled into my yard and saw Brent's car parked with his license plate labeled Mr. Town. "He's so corny." I laughed to myself. Getting out of the car and grabbing my bag of tacos, I grinned in anticipation. I'd stopped off at a taco hut because the salad made me even hungrier. What the girls didn't know wouldn't hurt. I placed my key into the door and walked inside. The TV was on full blast with Barney playing, while Brent lay on the couch with his shoes and shirt off, looking good enough to eat. I licked my lips, shaking my head with the dirty thoughts of us having sex again. Both my babies sat in a rocking chair, and sucking on their hands. I took my tennis shoes off, dropped my bag on the floor, and walked over, sitting on the opposite end of the couch.

"How was the workout?" he asked.

"Fine."

"So, it was good."

"Yep."

"You can't give me more than just one-word answers?" Brent said, rising and grabbing his shirt to put it on.

I shrugged, not answering. Whenever I was in his presence, I wanted to be his woman, and I knew my attitude was something I needed to work on. "Ugh, Brent, what do you want me to say? I worked out and caught up with my best friends, talking about the good old days. Stuff like how I need to find a man."

A crease in his forehead and his narrowed eyebrows told me I'd fucked up with talking about another man.

"Angela, don't get fucked up by having my girls calling another man Dad."

"You moved on, so why can't I?" I yelled, jumping out of my seat, startling my babies. They started crying. I dropped the taco bag and picked up Marcia, and he grabbed Jazmine, rubbing her back and kissing her cheek to calm her down. Watching him care for our babies tugged at my heart. He was so gentle, sweet, and calm. Way more natural at this parenting thing than I. Especially with changing diapers, the man had a stomach of steel.

"Why do you continue to play the victim? This relationship could have gone a different route. How many times have I told you I love you and would do anything to make you happy? But it starts from the inside, baby. The jealousy and vindictiveness eating away at you will overwhelm things if you let it and will prevent you from having a love that can last a lifetime, but you'll need to meet me halfway. I was dating on and off in California. Yes, she was someone I was seeing steadily, but I didn't claim her as my girlfriend."

"I'm not in the mood to deal with this. I need a shower and food. It was a long day and bickering back and forth is not what the girls need to see."

"Then take a shower and get your mind right because I'm not going anywhere. Elena is the past, and I've explained that to her and you. You wanted things between us to be strictly co-parenting, so that's what I committed to do."

"The one time you listen to what I say, and it's this," I muttered under my breath, walking off toward the twins' bedroom to place Marcia down.

"What was that?" he asked, following me.

I opened the door and walked inside their purple-and-yellow room. They loved Barney, and I remembered watching "Barney & Friends" when I was growing up, so I had the nursery decorated in purple with a big poster and shapes of the different characters hanging on the wall. I leaned over and placed Marcia down, and he laid Jazmine in her crib.

I stepped into my bedroom and pulled off my top and pants, throwing them in the hamper. I opened the drawer and pulled a large t-shirt and panties out. I could feel his eyes on me, but I refused to turn around. I headed toward the bathroom and opened the door, then closed it, turning the lock. I needed a moment to think and get my mind right. Starting a fight with him wasn't my intention but remembering that stupid text message, and her calling his phone, pissed me off. I turned the shower on and lathered up the soap, washing the tumultuous emotions of the day away.

I inhaled deeply before releasing a harsh breath. "Fuck, I love that asshole," I mumbled to myself as a tear pooled down my cheek.

Thirty minutes later, I stepped out of the shower and dried off. Hearing my TV playing in my bedroom. I quickly opened the door wearing just the towel around my body. He was laid out on my bed, propped up with the TV on, watching some Netflix Black Mirror show.

"Umm, what are you doing?"

"What does it look like?"

"That's my bed you have your nasty feet on," I sassed and pointed at his feet, walking over to turn the TV off.

He stared at me, licking his lips and smirking. That smirk always caused me to drop my panties, and I refused to give in—especially since I had five more weeks to go.

"My babies got you looking good, princess. That extra weight filled you out in all the right places."

"Shouldn't you give compliments to your girl and not me? Besides, I'm working on removing some of this baby weight and fast."

"Girl, you look good. Stop tripping and come sit down. We can at least be friends. We were at one time before the relationship part if you recall. I used to always make you laugh and bring you food and help you with your homework between classes." Brent chuckled, patting the seat next to him on the bed.

"Let me put on some clothes quick, and we can watch something together."

"I've seen all of you, Angela, and been all in your guts; there's nothing you can hide from me that I don't know about, sweetheart. Unless you're afraid that you'd be tempted to jump on me," Brent chortled.

I stuck my middle finger up at him and walked off in a huff to close the bathroom door and change.

Five minutes later, I came out and sat on the bed with my strawberry lotion and squirted a little in my hand to rub it on my legs. He snatched the lotion out of my hands and pulled my legs into his lap. Pouring a small amount into the palm of his hand, he rubbed up and down my ankles toward my inner thigh.

"I didn't need assistance," I moaned in a low, teasing voice as I closed my eyes and bit my bottom lip.

"Remember I used to do this for you in college after one of your many showers or our marathon sex sessions."

"Don't remind me. Somehow, we always ended up even dirtier right after," I whispered, allowing him to run a hand up my stomach that still held a small pouch from the birth of my babies and a faint black line.

"That was never our problem, Angela. Somehow, your insecurities about your parents always derailed your idea of what we could have had or been." He continued to blaze a trail up my body, stopping right before he touched my right breast. I wanted him to go farther, but the mood shifted at the mention of my parents. Then it transitioned into Kimberly's call earlier about my cousin dropping by the salon. Neither of those thoughts helped my mood. I moved out of his hold and stood, pissed off all over again.

"Can you go, please? I need to be alone."

"You got it, Angela. Kiss my babies for me, and I'll see you later." Brent sighed and walked out of my room.

I fell back on the bed, staring at the ceiling. I wiped the tears away from my eyes as the door shut, knowing he wouldn't be coming back to hold me.

Chapter Eight

Angela

The next day, my alarm went off late, and I was rushing to drop the girls off with Granny, since I planned to pop into the shop for a few hours and look over some paperwork. I turned the radio low as I looked back in the rearview mirror at my babies, still sleeping in their car seats. I'd forgotten to text Brent this morning; he made me promise to always text a photo of the girls every morning, so he'd know how they were doing. I guess because I hadn't done it yet, and it was going on nine AM, he was blowing me up.

I answered before he could wake the girls up. "They're fine, Brent," I snapped, annoyed at not only him, but the driver in front of me, who was taking forever to go through traffic when the light turned green. I blew my horn, and they still sat there, so I pulled around and drove off.

"Who are you honking at, Angela? You know you can't be speed racing with my babies in the car with you!" Brent yelled, shuffling around with background noise filtering in, sounding like a television.

Ignoring his yelling, I looked back again at my girls, and they both opened their eyes at the same time, yawning and smacking their little lips. They were the spitting image of their father with his dimples and button nose.

"Angela! Angela!" Brent snapped through the phone, right as I pulled up to Granny's house. I wanted to wait to bring the girls to my shop until they got a little older. Seeing as I would only be gone for a few hours, I didn't want to shuffle them back and forth in this weather; it was chilly during this time of the year in New York.

"What, Brent? Why are you yelling like I'm Elena or something? I'm not speeding, and I'm at Granny's house, dropping the girls off before I head into the shop."

"Watch your mouth, Angela. Let me see my girls on FaceTime," Brent said, agitated. He hung up and called back on FaceTime.

"Brent, I don't have time for you to be calling me at nine in the morning, like I don't have work to do. Once they get in the house with Granny, I'll have her call you. Now, goodbye," I muttered and hung up in his face. I threw the phone in my purse and took my keys out of the ignition. I heard the door open and looked up, seeing Pops in his normal blue-and-white-striped pajamas, coming outside to help me with the girls. I passed him the baby bags, and then pulled Jazmine out first. He took her in this left arm and walked inside. I shut the door and walked around to the other side, grabbed Marcia, and walked into the house. I smelled black coffee brewing, and Granny was sitting on the couch as Pops laid the car seat down in front of her, along with the diaper bag.

"I shouldn't be too long today. Mostly paperwork, and then I'll call when I'm on my way back." I bent down and kissed her on the cheek, and she nodded. "Be good for your grandparents, girls. Will you FaceTime Brent? He has the girls on a routine of afternoon Daddy-daughter time." I hurriedly kissed my babies and turned to leave as the next words out of Granny's mouth stopped me dead in my tracks for a second.

"I heard from your momma's side of your family."

"Okay."

The thought of them reaching out through Granny and Pops pissed me off even more because everyone knew those two were the only people who could make me do anything—besides my daughters.

"Angela, hear them out."

"Who exactly is reaching out to speak with me?"

"Some cousins on your mom's side. I didn't go too much into detail when she called. I think her name was Jessica or something."

"She's probably calling about needing some money or something. Anyway, I have enough problems as it is, without adding more family drama. I'll call before I head over to see if you need anything."

* * *

It was still early when I arrived at my shop, and it was already busy in the parking lot because of the nail salon and corner store next door. We all shared the parking spaces. The only open parking was next to someone who took up some extra room. I could already feel my annoyance at the rude driver for not being considerate of other business owners. And then I accidently bumped my door into the car that was covering two spots. "Damn it!"

Hearing my phone vibrate, I saw Brent's name come

across the screen. Ignoring him, I backed up, shut the door, and was about to walk off, when suddenly, the driver's side door opened, and a tall man—at least five-eleven—with a small goatee, heavy eyebrows under wide eyes, and a crooked smile turned toward me. "Were you about to walk off and not say anything?"

"No, I was going to leave a note," I explained, panicking and trying to make up an excuse to not have to pay for any damages.

He stood with his hands in his pockets and smirked at me with a knowing look that said *I know you're lying*. I walked around to the side of the door I hit and checked the spot. Running a hand across the handle, I didn't see any damage.

"Nothing is scratched."

He came around to stand behind me and bent down to check the same spot as I just did. Checking his door handle on his black BMW and then eyeing me up and down, I could see where this was going.

"I disagree."

I was tempted to run him over with my car, for wasting my time with this fake situation.

"You can't be serious right now. I barely even touched your door," I complained, crossing my arms across my chest and peering into his eyes.

"I'm Lincoln. You're Angela, right? The owner of the salon?" Lincoln said, waving his hand at my building.

"I don't care," I said and tried to walk off, only for him to walk in front of me, blocking the entrance.

"Angela, are you always this uptight?" Lincoln said, biting his lower lip and casting his gaze from my toes up to my low-cut, short tracksuit I decided to wear today with high heels and light makeup.

"Lincoln, are you always this desperate?" I countered with irritation, hoping he got the hint.

"Baby, I'm far from desperate, I assure you. You look like you're in a hurry, so I'll let you go and get back to work. Remember, you owe me for that scratch on my door," Lincoln said, right as a grey Lamborghini pulled into the parking space in front of our storefronts.

I already knew trouble was brewing whenever my babies' father was around. Brent turned the car off and got out, wearing grey jogging pants, a white t-shirt, and tennis shoes—not his normal business attire.

"What are you doing here, Brent?" I questioned, annoyed that he followed me to my place of business.

"What's up, Lincoln? How's the shop looking?" Brent asked, ignoring me completely and shaking hands with the rude Lincoln.

"Everything's good with the shop, man. How do you know little smart ass right here?" he said, chuckling at my mouth hanging wide open at his comment.

"That's my daughters' mother. We've known each other since middle school. How do you two know each other?" Brent questioned, and I walked off, shaking my head.

I headed inside, turned the lights on, and walked into my office. I flung my purse on the coat hanger and set my phone down. A few minutes later, Brent walked inside as I turned my computer on and sat at my desk.

"Stay away from him. Lincoln's the biggest hoe in New York, and I'd rather my baby momma didn't end up on the receiving end of his tales," Brent barked, shutting and locking my door in my office.

"Lincoln—or whoever he is—is the last thing on my mind. Why are you here? The girls aren't here." I glanced over at him as he moved about my office, looking at the plaques and photos of our kids and friends.

"You hung up on me." Brent walked over and turned my chair around, glowering down at me.

"I was busy, and I don't answer to you—unless your name is Jazmine or Marcia Townsend," I hissed, standing and poking my finger at his chest to make sure he understood that I was a grown woman and not his child. He waved off my words like they were mosquitoes.

"You should save that attitude for the person who deserves it, not me, princess." Brent sat on the couch in my office, picking up a magazine and thumbed through it. He was probably following me and knew the girls weren't here and wanted to get all in my business.

Should save that attitude. I mumbled under my breath and snatched the magazine out of his hand and stood in front of him as he stretched out with his feet propped on the table like this was his home away from home.

"I doubt you're making any money while you're stalking me, sir. I suggest you head to work instead of following me around," I sassed, dropping the magazine on the table and sitting on the edge of my desk with my legs crossed.

His eyes lowered and peered at my thick thighs. He shifted in his seat and bit his lower lip. "Anyway, I talked to Granny the other day, and she told me that your cousins have been trying to get in touch with you, but you've ignored their calls. I know that side of your family isn't the greatest, princess, but are you sure about keeping our kids away from them? Tomorrow, my family is celebrating my mom's birthday, and looking at how close my family is with the girls, I don't want you regretting that you're keeping them away," Brent said, sighing and rubbing a hand against my cheek.

Chapter Nine

Brent

Everyone who knew Angela didn't understand the real girl behind all that laughter, feistiness, and edginess. She played the role of a fierce lion in front of everyone, but she couldn't hide her true nature when she let her guard down and let herself be vulnerable. I knew not having her family in her life and being raised by her friend's family was a tough pill to swallow. The moment I saw her in class all those years ago, and she tried to flirt in front of everyone, and I turned her down; the look in her eye said it all. Rejection was something she didn't deal with very well.

"What time are we going to your parents' place tomorrow?" she asked, changing the subject.

"Six, and my mom said to just bring yourself and the girls. Don't try to bring any of Granny's food to hide and eat because you don't eat other folks' cooking," I said, following her and staring at her round, plump ass.

"I'm sorry, Brent, but your momma can't cook. The last time we had dinner at her place, I ended up with food poisoning. How do you expect me to take my daughters and not prepare myself? Plus, your crazy cousin gets on my nerves, thinking there's some sort of competition between us."

"Because you're always ragging on her husband and his toupee. Then you're up here talking about her lack of holding down a job," I stated, shaking my head and remembering all the times I had to separate my cousin and Angela from each other.

"Excuse me? You were the one who told me she's had twenty-two jobs within a year. You said she kept getting fired because she was either calling out and faking sick or sleeping with the boss." Angela shrugged, picking up the hamper of towels and passing me a box of empty spray bottles with her salon logo on them.

"Listen, just try to get along with my family, please. You really need to call your cousins. It won't hurt to put an effort into having extra family around."

She sat in the salon chair and huffed, blowing out a breath. "I guess you're right. Maybe I'll call them back tomorrow after dinner. Hope they're not looking for a handout because I refuse to be taken advantage of—especially with them barely taking an interest in our girls."

"All right, so, are we good now? No more fighting and pushing me away, princess? I come in peace. Can we be friends or—"

Angela raised her hand before I finished my statement. "Friends, and you have to keep your little girlfriend away from our kids. I'd hate to end up..."

"In jail. I know, you've said it a million times, princess. I did end things with Elena; she just hasn't come to terms with us being apart."

Right before she was about to speak, the door chimed, and her assistant walked inside. "Good morning, everyone. Hey, Brent. What are you doing here?" Kimberly asked, placing her purse on the desk.

I lifted the box of empty bottles, showing off the workload that Angela forced me into. "Helping your hot-in-the-pants boss not end up on Lincoln's Most Wanted list." I laughed at my own joke as Angela hissed through her teeth in annoyance.

"Please tell me you didn't go out with him?" Kimberly questioned, walking around the back area of her desk, removing her jacket, and turning on her computer. As she continued setting up her workspace, more people piled into the salon.

"That's my cue to head out before you ladies get to gossiping. Princess, I'll call you later when I'm on my way to your place tonight to see the girls."

Placing a kiss on her cheek, I dropped the box down next to her chair and waved to the rest of the stylists as I headed out, catching Lincoln talking on the phone.

"You heading out for the day, B?" Lincoln asked

"Yep, those million-dollar deals won't sell themselves. Before I go, let me talk to you for a minute, man to man."

He smirked, already knowing what would come out of my mouth. I didn't hesitate to fake how the situation would make me feel if Angela started dating—let alone dating Lincoln. Deep down, we both knew we'd get back together eventually. She just needed time to figure out if she was in for the long haul.

"What's up?"

"I won't say this any other way, and you know me. I speak my mind and mean what I say. Stay away from Angela. We both know she's too good for you. Besides, she's my daughters' mother."

"B, you tripping, man. I'm just trying to run my business, and she came at me. Going forward, I'll keep my eyes to myself," Lincoln answered and raised his hands in fake surrender.

"Yeah, the best thing for everyone is for you to stay focused on your business, and I'll stay focused on Angela and our kids," I told him without a hint of humor in my tone.

"I see, you're still in love—something I don't do with women."

"Love has nothing to do with this, Lincoln. You know as well as I do that Angela's too good for you, and as I recall, you're still dating my cousin. So again, how did you think this would play out?" I asked.

He stood, grinning in my face and rubbing his hands together. "I'm not married, and your cousin and I have a mutually beneficial arrangement."

"By that, you mean dating my ex and my cousin at the same time? You think both women would be okay with that arrangement? Motherfucker, you've lost your rabbit-ass mind."

"Come on, now. I'm just joking with you. I respect you, Brent. No hard feelings. I understand what you're saying, and I'll back off," he said, and I unclenched my fists, walking off toward my car.

I opened the door and stared as he walked into his shop and peered over at the salon. We both knew if he stepped out of line, we'd have a major problem.

Chapter Ten

Angela

There I was, sitting at Granny's house with my girls and staring at my phone. After the talk with Brent and calling Emery over for additional moral support, I decided to make the call I'd been dreading forever. I looked over at my little bundles of joy and wanted to protect them and keep harm away. The thought of someone not wanting to have them in their life broke my heart. I was determined not to make the same mistakes my mother made, and building a better relationship with Brent was the biggest change I was making in my life.

He was there, along with the other guys, watching the game. We decided to hang with our friends before heading over to his family's place.

"Angela, did you eat anything yet?" Emery asked, walking inside the dining room with a plate of pork chops and lasagna.

"No, because Brent made me promise I wouldn't eat anything before going to his parents' house," I explained, taking a bite of her pork chop as she sat beside me.

"Oh, well here, have my whole plate. So, you're calling your grandmother and cousins, right?"

Nodding in answer, I opened the unsaved text message and looked down at another text by my mother's mom, wanting to reconnect. I sent word through Granny that I needed time to think.

Mildred's Mother: *Hi, Angela. I know it's been awhile. I'd like to talk with you. I heard you had the babies.*

"So, you haven't responded to her since the day the girls were born?"

"Nope."

"Damn, is she that toxic of a person?"

"The little bit I remember, she was always yelling and fussing with my mom. Then my mom, of course, was always drinking and depressed over my dad after the divorce, so it was a spiraling effect. I guess seeing her daughter that empty was too much for her, and it made her leave us alone to the point my mom left me with you guys."

"Let me guess. She found out who your kids' father is and wants to be in their lives now?"

"Probably, but I wouldn't let her old ass anywhere near my babies. I do want to find out about some of my relatives. It's been a few years since we've talked," I replied, laying my head on her shoulder, tossing the phone down on the table.

"What are you two doing here? Hiding out from the fellas? Think y'all slick or something. I already told Pops I'm going to the casino tonight, and I refuse to babysit any longer."

"Didn't you just go to the casino a week ago with your church sisters?" Emery asked.

"Okay—and what does that have to do with today?

Little girl, don't question me. I raised *you*—not the other way around," Granny sassed, passing Jazmine over and placing her in my arms. She giggled and grabbed both sides of my face, leaving spit on my face.

"Eww! Jazmine, baby, you nasty! Who taught you to slobber on people, huh?" I chuckled, looking at her as she lit up with her dimples.

"She looks just like Brent. And a little mixture of you in the ears and eyes."

I nodded. "Getting heavy, little girl. Come on, let's go in the living room and mess with your daddy." I stood with Emery walking beside me, carrying Jazmine's blanket.

"Aww, come on, man. That was pass interference!" Brent yelled, jumping off the couch in frustration.

"How much longer is this game going to be on? Otherwise, we'll miss dinner at your parents', Brent." I wasn't feeling up to dealing with his batshit crazy family.

He grabbed Jazmine from my arms and kissed her lips, then kissed me on the cheek. I was a little taken aback by it and was momentarily stunned.

"We can go now since they're only in the third quarter. I'll catch the rest at my folks' house," Brent suggested.

"All right. Let me grab Marcia, change her diaper, and get her bag and my purse. Emery, I'll talk to you tomorrow after the dinner—and maybe after I call my long-lost relatives. I swear, this is some 'Days of Our Lives' type of shit." I rolled my eyes at my comment and chortled, bending down and grabbing the babies' bags and shoes.

* * *

I arrived at Brent's parents' house and saw his car parked outside. I texted for him to come out and help with the car seats. As I stuffed my phone in my purse, the front door opened, and he walked outside. He wore a pair of black jeans and a cream-colored, button-down shirt.

"Did you change clothes?"

"Yeah, I had a change of clothes in my car and came straight here. Why, what's wrong?"

Usually, he didn't dress up to hang with his parents—unless he had a date with someone else. *What am I saying? He's not crazy enough to go out on a date, and then make me come here to pretend in front of his family*, I thought snarkily.

He opened the driver's side door, and I stepped out. He pulled me into his arms and kissed my forehead, then my cheek.

I clung to his chest and relaxed into his arms. "You smell good; is that a new cologne?" I inquired, wondering whether he'd changed up his routine for a certain person or for me.

Brent ran a hand over his low-cut hair and smirked at me. He knew I was lowkey interrogating him to get answers. "Stop being nosy and come on, so we can get this dinner going. I know what you're trying to do, and causing a fight won't get you out of this family dinner. Nice try though," he said with a wink.

"I have no idea of what you're talking about." I reached out to grab the baby bags as he picked up Jazmine's car seat first, then Marcia's. I'd decided to only bring a few items with us tonight, so we could get in and out as fast as possible.

Chapter Eleven

Brent & Angela

"Angela, sweetie, how does the eggplant parmesan taste? It's my new recipe I've been trying out," Mother asked.

I watched as she poked around the plate, trying to give a hint that she wasn't hungry. But seeing her narrowing eyes and my cousin glaring, waiting for me to commit, I cleared my throat and tried to keep the peace.

"Good, did you make this today?" Angela asked.

"I did, fresh out of the oven right before you guys came," Mom answered, passing her another piece and offering me one. I nudged the plate away that I was full.

"Yep, she made about four different versions before this one came out right," Donate, my brother-in-law, joked.

His wife slapped him across the chest for joking at her expense. Brent and I couldn't help but laugh as his mom ignored what he said and continued eating her food.

"How is everything at the salon, Angela? I heard you're looking to expand?" Brent's cousin asked. She'd grown up around me, and we were extremely close, like

66

her and Emery. Her parents were in and out of her life up until about five years ago, but that was because they were both in the Army. I would have thought she would have made something of herself with parents who had committed their lives to serving their country, but Brianna was a known manipulator. She was spoiled and jealous, and there were many times she tried to break up our relationship.

Taking a sip of my water to clear my throat of the large piece of tomato that clogged my esophagus. I wiped my mouth with the napkin on the table, curious where this conversation may go.

"The salon is good. Why do you ask?" Angela replied.

Brianna popped her lips and rolled her neck with an attitude, clearly with an agenda.

"Because you're always leaving your kids with my cousin or your grandmother who's not really family, rather than bring them over here," Brianna sassed.

"Are you mad, Brianna? Brent, what have you been telling your family?"

"Brianna, don't start. We've had a lovely dinner tonight, and you're already starting this," I groaned, rubbing a hand down my face in frustration. He tried to reach for my hand, and I snatched it away, pissed that she even had the audacity to question me about my kids.

"Brent didn't have to say anything to me; we noticed the lack of calls, and the number of photos getting posted on your social media with your family. Those girls are half of my blood. Oops, my bad—the fake family you claim as blood." Brianna chuckled, standing like she was ready to fight.

"So, Mrs. Townsend, how are things at the church? Brent's always bragging about how much you volunteer and give back to your community. I've been meaning to set up a spa day type of thing for the single moms," Angela said, effectively squashing the subject before things could get ugly.

"Things at the church are doing great, and I see your grandparents all the time," my mother answered.

"Those aren't her *real* grandparents," Brianna mumbled under her breath, rolling her eyes.

"Why do you care so much about who her family is, Brianna?" I said through gritted teeth. I narrowed my eyes as I tried to keep myself calm.

"Because she's using you for your money—the same way she used the Stone family. Everyone in town knows your track record with men. Hope your daughters don't turn out like you."

"Brianna! Keep my daughters' names out of your mouth and shut up! What we're *not* going to do is have a back and forth in front of my kids! Show some damn respect!" I shouted, slamming my hand on the table and surprising everyone with my sudden burst of anger.

* * *

ANGELA

If I weren't so annoyed with him constantly talking about me to his family about our problems, that outburst would have had me ready to marry him, but his little performance only validated that I would always have to fight to get some type of respect within his circle of friends and family because I wasn't the type of woman they expected him to be with—like the women in his family. They mostly took care of the home, and I'd never had a desire to want the lifestyle they presented as "loving." Granny kept me updated on all the gossip down at the church, and the Townsend family wasn't exactly what you might call squeaky clean like they tried to make themselves out to be.

"Let her keep talking, Brent. Obviously, she'd held some things inside and feels hurt. Why? I haven't the slightest clue, since I have kids by *you* and not her," I said, waiting to see her next move.

"Aunt and Uncle tolerate you, Angela, and they won't speak up, since their son loves your dirty-thong ass, but *I'm* more than willing to keep him from making another mistake with you," Brianna taunted.

I chuckled at her trying to call me out and put my business on blast. Brent already knew what type of woman I was as we got older and went off to college. I would never apologize for how I led my life, and for her to try to demean me in front of my children was the final straw.

"Brianna, sit and leave it alone. We're happy that Brent is happy; that's all that matters," his father spoke up, finally trying to deescalate the tension in the room.

Marcia cried in her seat, and I leaned over to place her pacifier back in her mouth. Brent attempted to help, and I jerked back, pissed that this dinner was turning out exactly like I knew it would.

"Everyone needs to just calm down. Brianna, stay out of their business and focus on your own relationships," Brent's mother said, pouring more lemonade in her husband's cup.

Brianna's boyfriend—or husband. I could barely remember his name, since she changed men like she changed underwear—stood to pull her into her seat and calm her down, as Brent's father shrugged his shoulders and pulled a cigar out of his breast pocket. Mrs. Townsend yanked it out of his hand and pointed toward the kids in the room. Brent shook his head, and I giggled under my breath. He reached over and rubbed a hand down my thigh. His touch helped calm me down for a second.

"Another thing: My cousin was happy with Lauren, but your issues kept him from moving on and being happy," Brianna pointed out. "Then, he found love with Elena."

"Brianna, stay out of our business. Are you the spokesperson for all Brent's exes? Damn, how about you focus on *your own* situation." I pointed at her man, texting away on his phone and smiling.

She looked over at what had my attention and snatched the phone out of his hand.

"Brianna, baby, hold up; that's business!" her husband shouted, wrestling to get the phone from her, but she stuck it in her bra.

Chapter Twelve

Angela

Brianna wanted a fight, and I wasn't in the mood to give it to her this time. I'd matured a little over the months since I'd had my babies. One thing I wouldn't do was jeopardize losing them.

"Brianna, I suggest you take a seat and leave grown folks' business alone," I chastised, leaning over the table with my fists, ready to go. "Who am I kidding? I'm always ready to fight."

"Brianna, nobody is fighting, and I told you that stuff in confidence before Angela and I made up," Brent said, pulling me to sit back down.

Yanking out of his hold, I glared and sat back down since our girls were staring a hole in the side of my face.

"Brent, you don't have to answer to her. You should have stayed with Elena, at least she was cuter," Brianna joked, strutting off to the kitchen. I tried to jump and run after her, but Brent gripped my arm tight.

"Princess, calm down. She's just testing you," Brent whispered and kissed my cheek.

"She shouldn't have to test me if you'd stand up for

me with your family. The story you told must have been good if she already hates me."

"Brianna has nothing better to do than cause problems, baby. Don't let her get you out of character," Brent suggested, gripping my chin gently and kissing my lips.

"How much longer do we have to be here? I need to get the girls home and bathed." I was over this little happy family dinner, and the food wasn't helping. His mom brought out another dish that smelled like burnt socks, and Brianna was right behind her with something that looked like meatballs wrapped in green lettuce. "Mrs. Townsend, I'm not feeling well. If you don't mind, I need to take off early. Brent can stay if he'd like with the girls, but my stomach isn't wanting to hold anything down," I said, creating a whole story to get out of this night.

"Oh, sorry you're not feeling well. Are you sure you don't want to take a plate to go? Or maybe rest upstairs in one of the guest rooms?" Mrs. Townsend offered, making me feel bad for always ragging on her food—not enough to *stay* but enough to feel sorry for doing it behind her back.

Shaking my head, I kissed both my girls and Brent on the cheek.

He followed me and walked me to my car. "You know, you're wrong about this," Brent chortled, opening the driver's side door.

"Sorry, but I can't do another second of your mother's food, or your cousin and her stank attitude. I would question you about what you've told her, but I'm trying to move in a positive direction in my life."

"I hear you, Angela, but baby, you can't be mad because of how I felt about the situation. We need to continue to communicate—and maybe leave other people out of our relationship."

"What relationship?"

"Girl, get home safe and call me once you make it. I'll have the girls home after we have dessert."

"Don't feed my babes none of that mess!" I yelled through the window as he headed back inside and waved me off.

Driving off into traffic, I clicked on my Bluetooth in the car to call Emery and Jordan together. Hopefully, they could make sense of the entire situation without me wanting to lay my hands on his family member.

"What's up, Angela?" Emery mumbled through a moan. I heard rustling over the line, and I almost wanted to call back, but this was a girlfriend moment.

"Hello, besties!" Jordan sang into the phone.

"Ew, Emery, are you fucking?" I called her out. "Tell Jackson to leave you alone for a second. Can't you two be in a room together and not have sex, like normal married couples?"

"That's your problem. Now that you're not getting any sex, you're driving everyone else crazy," Emery retorted and whispered for Jackson to give her a few minutes alone. I heard him bark that he needed an extra blowjob in the morning to make up for the interruption.

"I promise I will, baby," Emery mumbled away from the line, then said into the phone, "All right, why are you bothering me when you should be having dinner with your in-laws?"

"We got into a fight—well, *almost* a fight—because of his cousin Brianna," I said, pulling up to the light. I saw a text from Brent.

Future Ex-Husband: *Sorry about how the evening went. I'll make it up to you.*

"A fight!" Emery and Jordan shouted at the same time.

"What did you do?" Jordan asked.

"Not a thing, I promise. You guys would have been proud of me. I showed up somewhat late. I lost track of time, fiddling around with the girls and Granny. Brianna's the one who started everything. Brent decided to put our business on Front Street and told her everything about our situation."

"Huh," Emery muttered, sounding like she was in the bathroom.

"Are you taking a shit? While we're on the phone with you?" I questioned. She was the type of friend who didn't care about boundaries. Yes, I might take a bra off or change clothes in front of my friends, but Emery didn't care and would leave the door of the bathroom open if she was peeing and needed to talk to you at the same time.

"Worry more about the fight and less about what I'm doing."

"I mean, she kind of has a point, Emery; you do weird things like that," Jordan said, backing me up and calling Emery out on her shit—literally.

"I can hang up right now if you'd like and let Jordan help you with your little problem. I'm *not* shitting, if you must know. I was gathering my toothbrush to get ready for dinner."

"Tell that lie to somebody else, child. Anyway, what do I do about Brent's family? Because we'll be in each other's lives for the next eighteen years."

"Tell Brent to keep Brianna out of your relationship and focus on what you two can build together without any outside influence. He's still trying to feel you out, Angela, so I can't blame him for being a little hesitant with his feelings and confiding in Brianna and his parents," Emery said as I pulled into my parking space outside my house and turned the car lights off.

Grabbing my purse and keys, I switched the call from Bluetooth back to my phone, stepped out of my car, and headed inside, placing my keys on the TV stand and taking a seat on the couch.

"I agree with Emery on this one, Angie. Talk with Brent and explain your feelings without making the entire dinner a bigger issue, so we won't end up having to do back-and-forth arbitrary pickups for the kids again," Jordan said.

I grunted, annoyed that my friends knew how I would have handled the situation if I hadn't called and decided to be an adult and talk things over first. But if Brent let things escalate with his cousin again, then I knew how to handle her—and next time, I'd have a taser.

Chapter Thirteen

Angela

The last thing I wanted was for Brent's family to think I was some crazy baby momma. So, after much more discussion and calling Brent back and forth, I let his mom see the girls for a few hours today. Then I picked them up to bring them with me to the shop. I knew Brent was busy with work, and I didn't want to hound Granny or Emery. I only had three clients today and mostly paperwork, so it wouldn't be too long of a day.

"Angela! Angela!" my client shouted, breaking me out of my stare.

"Sorry, I have mommy brain and can't seem to turn it offten."

"No worries. How are things with Brent and co-parenting?" she inquired, turning the page of the new *Essence* magazine with Serena Williams on the cover.

"Things are decent. We have a routine and the girls on a schedule. Early on in the beginning, I kind of let Emery handle things with dropping them off to him. Now, we've gotten better with our communication and built our friendship back up."

"So, he's forgiven you for keeping the pregnancy a secret?"

"I mean we've briefly talked about it in the past, but I think we're past that now."

"Wasn't he dating some model chick out here?"

"He said it was just a fling, you know how men are. I don't care as long as he takes care of my girls. He can date whoever he chooses," I said, lying through my teeth.

"Ouch! Angela, you burnt my ear, girl."

"Damn, sorry, girl. Half off today."

"Half off! How about free? Damn, my ear hurts. Let me use the restroom and check it out."

"Ugh, yeah, use the one in my office." I pulled my phone out of my pocket and texted Brent. I had a funny feeling I couldn't shake.

Me: *Where are you?*

Future Ex-Husband: *Work, why?*

Me: *Nothing. Just curious to see if you'd be stopping by later today to see the girls.*

Future Ex-Husband: *Of course, princess.*

Me: *Stop calling me that.*

Future Ex-Husband: *What are you wearing?*

Me: *Nothing and waiting on Lincoln to come and take it off.*

Future Ex-Husband: *Casket.*

Me: *What is a casket?*

Future Ex-Husband: *What you'll be standing over in a new black dress, which you'll need once I kill him if he tries to step to you.*

I laughed aloud with tears in my eyes as my client came back from the bathroom to sit back down in my chair. I closed out of my messages and put my phone back into my pocket.

"What's with the giggles, Angela? You almost burnt my ear off."

"I said I was sorry."

"You must have talked to Brent? Only way you're smiling and cheesing because no other man can have you looking like that without spending money."

I waved off her comment. Unbeknownst to a lot of people, I never looked at Brent for his money. I honestly loved him because he made me feel protected and loved—even above all my messiness.

"Okay, enough about me and my lack of a love life. What's going on with you?"

Candy sat back further into my chair, and we continued talking about the lack of good men and our kids. The next few hours would end the same way as usual, with me at home, watching my girls sleep with poop everywhere.

* * *

I couldn't believe I let Granny talk me into coming to church bingo night, while the girls stayed with Emery's parents. The crowd was huge, with old and young people laughing and talking together. I paid the five-dollar fee and walked behind her as we moved toward her favorite spot in the front. Everyone knew she sat there—something she always told me whenever the bingo night came up in conversation.

"The church has to be raking in a lot of money from this gambling sin," I joked.

An older lady sat next to me, wearing a head wrap

and an "All I Do is Win" t-shirt, with candles sitting in front of her like she was practicing a ritual that would magically help her win. She rolled her eyes, and I rolled mine back and stuck my tongue out.

"Rude," the older woman said and moved her chair closer to a group of young guys.

"Angela, don't embarrass me in front of my church members. You said you needed a break, and I allowed you to hang with me tonight, but I will kick you out if you cause a problem," Granny scolded and passed me the bingo board.

"That's funny, because I recall you begging me to come because your partner, Gloria, wasn't feeling well tonight. Don't try to pull that guilt trip on me, old lady," I stated, and she gave me that look that all mothers and grandmothers gave their child when they'd done wrong and waited for them to apologize before they got an ass-whooping.

"Sorry," I mumbled under my breath.

"I thought so," Granny said.

The deacon announced the first row of numbers, and the game started without a hitch. We played a few rounds until about ten o'clock, and then called it a night when Pops called and told her to come home.

Chapter Fourteen

Brent

I finished up texting with Angela, and I knew after the dinner at my parents' place—and now, meeting up with Elena—I would have to do a lot to get back into Angela's good graces. The entire week, she was hot and cold with me, either having the kids dropped off at my place or having Granny's as the preordained meetup spot. After today, one way or another, this shit was going to end with us back together and Elena out of my life for good.

The guys told me about this new Mediterranean spot, and I knew Elena wouldn't be caught dead in a regular Denny's or Wendy's, so I planned a lunch at an expensive place to get her mind off what I was about to do.

As soon as I placed my menu down, I smelled a faint hint of lavender perfume. Elena grinned, walking up with the hostess behind her, who laid her menu down. Elena came around to kiss me on the lips. I turned before it landed, and she glared at me.

"Is that how we are now, Brent?" Elena asked, sitting and reaching out to entwine our hands.

"Elena, I'm not here for that. I told you we needed to talk, and you're not helping with all your bullshit calls and text messages." I snatched my hand away, and she frowned.

"Brent, you know as well as I do that we break up and make up all the time. Honey, just a few months ago, I had you screaming my name with your dick down my throat, so excuse me if I'm a little confused by this sudden end to a relationship that we both wanted," Elena spat, slamming her hand on the table.

I leaned over the table to close the space between us so only she could hear what I had to say. "You and I only have a friends with benefits, no strings attached type of relationship and nothing more. We barely talked about commitment, so spare me the little cries about us talking about a relationship."

"She's just going to hurt you again. How many times do you want to be her lap dog. The bitch can't even tell you she loves you!" Elena yelled. Standing suddenly, her chest heaved up and down erratically.

"Listen to me clearly because you've obviously taken this sleeping arrangement a little too far. I don't want you and never will. Angela is the mother of my kids and my future wife, so I suggest you leave both of us alone."

"I don't accept that, Brent. You made me love you, and now you're throwing me away because she decided to grow up and get a backbone," Elena whispered, agitated that I wasn't listening. Rather, I was checking to make sure everyone wasn't hearing her outburst.

"Calm down before you get us kicked out of here."

"No! I want you to come back to me now, and we can have kids and the house, and the whole American dream, baby."

My eyes bulged out at her talking about having kids.

"Are you out of your mind? I don't want kids with you, and this conversation is over. Stay away from Angela, my family, and me. Order whatever you like; lunch is on me as a parting gift," I said, taking my wallet out of my pocket and leaving a hundred-dollar bill on the table. At first, I'd thought we could talk like normal adults. Clearly, she had other plans.

* * *

I walked into Angela's place, and she was on what sounded like a three-way call with Emery and Jordan.

"Yeah, I talked to them, and we're planning on meeting up soon. Let me call you back. Brent just walked in, looking pissed off. I'm not giving him head! I told you that one time I pissed him off and gave him head, he forgot the reason he was mad in the first place. Girl... Emery, shut up! Oh, my God! Whatever. Call me later. Bye."

Placing my keys down on her coffee table, I lay on the couch with my feet up on her legs.

"Tough day?"

Rubbing my temple, I felt a migraine coming on. Nodding in answer, I asked, "Where my babies at?"

"In their room sleeping. Where are you coming from?" Angela questioned, helping to take off my shoes and rub my feet.

"Work."

"Stressful day at work, huh?"

"Yeah, how about your day?" I pried, changing the subject and pulling her down onto my chest.

"It was busy; I had the girls with me at the salon.

Then, I talked with some of my family members on my mom's side."

"That's great, babe," I said rubbing up and down her back. She laid her head on my chest and wrapped an arm around my waist.

"This is nice."

"What?"

"The two of us in one place with my kids upstairs sleeping." She pulled back, looking at me curiously. I pinched her cheek, smiling.

"You're so corny. You know that, right?" Angela ran a hand over my head and leaned up, meeting me halfway as I kissed her lips.

"I have no problem being corny for you and my girls. I need us to be on the same page, navigating together and in a healthy place as one unit. I love my parents, along with Granny and Pops, but we can't continue to use them as crutches in our relationship," I explained, rubbing her butt.

"Honestly, our lives have changed so much. I can't help but think something will come along and mess it up."

I pulled her against my chest and laced our hands together. "Remember when we were in school, and you tried to flirt with me in front of the class?"

She grinned mischievously as my hand ran up her shirt and pinched her nipple. "I recall you playing hard to get, and then once all the other boys showed me attention, you came running back to me," Angela whimpered under my hold as I moved her between my legs.

"Angela, your memories are different from what I recall. Maybe we should call Emery to help jog your memory, baby," I whispered, trailing kisses down her neck and across her shoulders.

"Emery will stick up for you... mmm-hmm, yes... right there, baby."

"Take off these clothes, so I can properly show you how I expect to please you for the next fifty years."

"Okay," Angela moaned, as we both hurriedly got undressed.

After talking with her cousins and finally coming to peace with her family and her abandonment issues, we were finally in the place where we could move forward together. Nothing would be perfect overnight, but I could see in her eyes she wanted what we could have... what Emery and Jackson had.

"I'm ready to see what happiness feels like. I can't say I won't have moments of doubt. Getting my feelings out has helped me to grow to be a little more confident in who I'm becoming," Angela muttered, kissing me deeply.

Chapter Fifteen

Angela

Brent slid in and out as his gaze raked over my body, his hands roaming my extra thickness from having two kids. I clawed at his thighs from behind, with sweat beading down my face. With my eyes closed, I enjoyed the closeness. There was tingling in pit of my stomach. "Baby, ugh... fuck," I mumbled into the pillow, stifling my screams to keep the noise level down, since the girls were sleeping.

The sound of his voice near my ear, whispering how much he loved me, caused me to get wetter. He'd found my vibrator earlier when I was cleaning and accepted the challenge to make me come with not only his dick, but my vibrator as well. Yanking it out of the nightstand, he turned it on and leaned over my back, not stopping his thrusts.

"What's the answer?"

Brent gradually moved the vibrator over my nipples, using his hands to play with my clit.

"Please, Brent! I can't!" I shouted, trying to push him away.

He pulled out abruptly and turned me around. He stood over me, stroking his dick. The very air around him seemed electrified. I'd never had a man please me the way he did. He moved the vibrator toward my pussy, along with his tongue. Suddenly, I felt my toes curl, and my body convulsed.

"I can't hear you, baby," Brent said and smacked his hand gently against my pussy as my juices poured down my thigh.

"Yes, you're my king, the best I ever had," I said, moaning. Mu body craved his hands.

His vitality still captivated me after all these years. I normally tapped out after two rounds, but we were on round four with my three orgasms to his one. Warm hands moved up my thighs to my hips and over my stomach. Entering me again, his strokes were slow and deliberate.

"Damn, princess, you feel so good." Brent's tongue ran over my left and then right breast, biting and licking my nipples. Unable to stop myself, I wrapped my legs around his back and pulled him in closer, as deep as he could get. "You feel just like you did in college, baby."

His raw, sensual prowess carried me to greater heights. "You too, baby," I moaned as my walls throbbed.

"Shit, Angela!" Brent picked up his pace, no longer using the vibrator. Our hearts hammered from the full weight of our lovemaking.

"Aghhh..." We came at the same time as he squeezed me in close, releasing his sperm into my womb. He fell next to me, and we struggled to control our breathing.

The girls started crying, and I turned over to get up. Brent motioned for me to stay in bed, and he'd get up to check on them. He put his boxers and jeans back on, walking out of the room to the bathroom to wash his hands and face. He headed out of the room, and I stayed in the fetal position as he placed a warm towel on my swollen pussy. I jerked back from the warmth and let him wipe me. He placed the towel in the hamper and headed toward the girls' room.

I was afraid I was making a mistake by giving into what could possibly be a new beginning for us. I couldn't let my heart get broken again. When he was engaged to Lauren, I'd put myself out there to get him back, and he'd turned me down. Now that he wasn't with Elena anymore, I needed to walk slowly with my eyes wide open. I had two little girls who depended on me. They and my business were my priorities.

Dragging myself out of bed, I went into the bathroom to turn on the shower and get dressed for the day. I had a full day of hair appointments and meeting my cousins for lunch. I put my hair in a ponytail, tested the water, and stepped inside. Seeing the hickeys Brent left, I shook my head and chuckled; he was marking his territory, a warning to other guys.

A cool breeze came across my back, and I felt eyes drift over me like a lover's caress as he stepped inside, grabbing the soap and towel out of my hand to wash my back.

"Was she hungry?" I asked, looking over my shoulder at Brent.

He leaned down to kiss my shoulder and then pulled me in close. "She needed her Pampers changed and to eat. The nanny got here, and I passed her over to feed her while I got dressed," Brent answered.

"What time do you have to be at work?"

"I have a meeting with a new client in an hour. Afterwards, we can do lunch with the girls if you want." His large hand lifted my face and held it gently.

I stood on my toes and encircled my arms around his neck. "I have back-to-back clients today. Plus, Renell and Jessica want to meet for lunch, and they invited Emery and Jordan."

"I know you talked to Granny about finding your long-lost family. I'm glad you're getting to know them." His tongue traced the soft fullness of my lips, and then he placed a gentle kiss across my forehead.

"Me, too. They came into the shop and explained who they were and asked if I wanted to get to know them. Jessica didn't push, and Renell reminded me of myself. So, that was a plus. They didn't harp on the situation with my parents."

Brent turned the water off and stepped out of the shower. He grabbed a towel and wrapped it around his waist, then picked up another one and waited for me to walk into his arms. He dried me off and kissed my shoulder blades.

* * *

My mind burned with memories of my mom and dad, cooking dinner in the kitchen, listening to Al Green's "Love and Happiness" while dancing. I was listening to Renell and Jessica, laughing about their latest dating shenanigans and being glad that dating wasn't still on my radar, between having two kids, working, and dealing with Brent and my situation—or relationship.

"Angela, what do you think?" Jessica wondered about my opinion on a new dress she wanted to buy.

"Ugh, that's cute," I replied.

"So, you think wearing a black negligee to a first date is good?" Jessica questioned.

All the girls chuckled, and I stared at the photo and giggled. "Sorry, boo; my mind's all over the place, but if you're feeling the guy, then it couldn't hurt to have it as a backup plan," I said, shrugging my shoulders and taking a sip of my green-tea lemonade.

Jessica had picked out the restaurant her uncle owned —and I guess he was my uncle, too, since he was my mom's brother. I'd heard about Margaret's Soul Food back in the day but didn't know it was a family business.

"When Angela has sex on her mind, you know she's just had some dick; you have to excuse her," Emery chortled, taking a scoop of my sweet potatoes. She'd ordered a salad, and Jordan was eating pasta with white sauce and a salad. Renell popped her lips and danced in her seat.

"Sexy, sexy, sexy, damn. If I didn't already have a crazy man at home, I'd take him out and put this good loving on him," she said, waving at the two gentlemen who had just walked into Margaret's in black tailored suits, chuckling at Renell's outlandish behavior.

"Girl, you know Jerry will kick your ass if you cheat on him," Jessica informed. Renell laughed to control her annoyance.

"Is Jerry your boyfriend or husband?" I inquired.

"If you ask him, we're married, but he's just my baby daddy. We've dated for over fifteen years and have a ten-year-old son. I gave up on trying to get him to walk down the aisle." Renell's voice was gritty with frustration. All the girls nodded in understanding.

Suddenly, a strong whiff of burnt eggs meant to be cologne came to the edge of our table. "I thought that was you, Angela," Morris said, leaning down. He wore a gaudy gold watch and two diamonds in each ear. I'd completely forgotten about Morris after our first date. He had been so selfish in bed and only lasted two minutes. I'd avoided him for over four years, and now, here he was, standing there in front of me, looking the same.

"How are you, Morris?" Emery asked.

He shot her a penetrating look and licked his lips. That was another reason it wouldn't work out with Morris —his flirtation with every woman he came across.

"No offense, Morris, but I'm having a private conversation." Annoyed with his presence, I covered my nose from the repugnant smell. He'd shown me who he was years ago, and I'd stopped taking his calls; no amount of money could have gotten me to date him again.

"Angie, you don't remember the good times, baby?" Morris asked, pinching my cheek.

"Morris, we went out on one date and had sex— which, if I recall, didn't last more than five minutes. So, to answer your question, I remember, but "good" wasn't exactly the word I would use to describe it," I answered and waved him off.

He hovered over our table for a few minutes as the girls snickered, then he turned and mumbled, "Bitch," under his breath and sat back down at his own table.

"Angela... did you have to hurt his feelings like that?" Jordan passed her plate over to the waitress, and I nodded.

"Yep. So, let's get back to Jessica's dating life—and away from mine."

Chapter Sixteen

Brent

Elena didn't take my breaking things off so easily, and she showed up at my office. She consistently called and left messages with my secretary, stating it wasn't over, or she was going to put the news out to the public that we were getting married unless I met with her. She even went so far as playing on Angela's phone.

"Brent, I understand you have kids with this person, but we were good together, honey." Elena seductively released her jacket. Underneath, she wore a long, thin, black dress that showed every curve. She sat on the edge of my desk, and her breasts pointed right at me, as though she'd gotten them done. I hoped she didn't think that would impress me.

She'd shown me once she couldn't be trusted, and not respecting what I was building with Angela and constantly interrupting my home life with my girls was a big red flag. Instead of letting her flirt any further, I moved her off my desk and stood her up.

"Elena, I told you it's over between us. I wasn't that

into you and your superficial lifestyle. Listen, I'm happy with my girl and my kids. You've shown me time and time again that I can't trust you."

"What did I do to make you think I wasn't trustworthy?"

"A few of my clients saw you in various states of undress during the time we were supposed to be together. I mean, I guess this is the second time a woman I spent time with wasn't committed to me—but at least *she* didn't cheat."

"Brent, I told you that wasn't me. Someone doctored those photos. Please, just give me another chance." Elena tried to kiss my lips, and I swerved out of her grasp.

"I'm with someone now."

"Who?"

"Angela," I answered, irritated at her stupid questioning.

"You sure weren't thinking about her when I had your dick in my mouth. Brent, she dumped you and left you broken, and I put you back together."

"Actually, *Lauren* helped put me back together. Then we broke up, and I started seeing you," I reminded her.

Silence lingered between us, and I wondered if she'd get the hint and leave my family alone before anything escalated. I knew it was bad enough to have lied about having to meet with a big client today, and Elena was here. I needed to get her out of here before Emery showed up and called Angela.

"There were many nights in California, you promised to love me and marry me. Did you forget about that? Huh! That girl doesn't want you, Brent. She's using you for your money!" Elena roared and stepped forward, hitting my chest with her balled-up fists.

I gently pushed her hands away, and she fell backwards in a huff. "I'm done talking about my relationship with you. It's a moot point, and I encourage you to focus on your career. What happened with that, anyway?"

With a roll of her eyes, she huffed and stomped to sit on the couch and poured herself a drink of water. "My agent says I need to focus more on doing editorial and not runway. I said I'd take a few months off and get back to him once I made my decision," Elena responded nonchalantly.

"Okay, well good luck with that, but I have real appointments that I need to prepare for and a conference call with a new client."

Elena smirked, lay back on the couch, and rolled the end of her dress up, showing off her pink thong. Right as I was about to tell her to cover up, Emery busted through the door.

"Brent, did you have..." Emery started to ask and dropped the folders in her hands.

"Emery, it's not what it looks like."

"It's exactly what it looks like, and you can tell your friend he's my man." Elena's smile widened in glee at the thought of Angela possibly finding out. I scratched the back of my neck nervously at trying to explain what was plain as day, a woman fucking herself on my couch in my office.

"Angela is going to kill you, Brent," Emery said harshly, looking between Elena and me.

"I didn't sleep with her, Emery. You know me better than that."

"Not yet anyway," Elena giggled and licked her fingers clean.

"Eww, please tell me you weren't about to sleep with

this thing," Emery said and folded her arms over her chest.

I stepped over to my desk and buzzed for security to escort Elena out of my office. A few minutes went by, and a knock at the door sounded with security asking how they could help. They yanked Elena up by her arm to escort her out of the building before Angela saw her and assumed something happened.

"Wait a minute, Brent. We're not done talking!" Elena screamed and tried to beat up the security guards.

For the next five minutes, it was complete silence in the office, and I knew Emery was ready to go off on me—until Angela walked inside, smiling brightly.

I breathed a sigh of relief; they'd just missed each other by a scant second. Having her show up unannounced again would have been a huge red flag for Emery, so I needed to contact security immediately and have them keep a look out.

Determined to keep my little situation away from prying eyes, I pleaded with Emery, with a gaze not to say anything that would push Angela away from what we were building. It wasn't perfect, but I wasn't cheating on her, either. The second she thought Elena was there—no matter the context—we'd be ten steps back to the beginning.

Emery must have felt the tension in the air and nodded to indicate that she would let Elena's presence go and act as though everything was perfectly okay. Her shoulders relaxed, and she peered at Angela, smiling after a few seconds.

Chapter Seventeen

Angela

I had already promised my cousins I would hang out with the rest of my family again. Opening myself up to meet the rest of my mom's side was new for me. It was all because of Granny and Brent, supporting me through it and not letting my anger over the past keep my daughters from knowing their family.

Once lunch was over, after seeing Morris, I needed to be in the arms of my man. I decided to surprise him with lunch—and possibly, a little midday desk romp. That would keep a smile on my face.

Breaking the rules, I walked right in and saw Emery and Brent having a staring contest. She had an angry glare across her face, with her foot tapping impatiently on the floor and her chest heaving up and down. Something was wrong, and I didn't like my best friends not getting along.

I shut the door behind m and waved the bag of food. Placing it on the table near the couch, I smelled a sweet scent that was somewhat familiar, or so I thought. Shaking it off, I smiled and slid my hands up Brent's chest, kissing his cheek.

"Anyone want to tell me what's going on?" I asked. The intense stare off seemed to end, and Emery smiled finally and shook her head.

"Girl, you know Brent and I can't come to an agreement on this latest deal with Foster's Jewelry. He wanted a two-year extension, and I implied it wasn't worth even re-signing them," Emery said, obviously keeping the real reason she was pissed to herself.

I played along and nodded. In time, the truth would be revealed.

"Yeah, babe, you know how I get about my money. Anyway, what brings you here today? We didn't have a scheduled date, did we?" Brent questioned, looking through his calendar on his desk.

"Nothing scheduled, and I was just in the neighborhood after the lunch with my cousins. I decided that before I went into the salon today, I wanted to see my man again," I cooed, laying my head on his shoulder, playing with his necktie.

"Well, I'll just give you two some privacy—and Brent, remember what we talked about. Some things are best to let go, since the return on the investment is worthless," Emery stated and walked out of the office.

I kind of felt like that was a slight at our relationship, but I knew she wouldn't be talking about us—even though Emery could be as shady as me at times.

Brent sat on the edge of his desk and pulled me into his arms, cocking his head to the side. "What's up, baby? I'm a little busy today," Brent said.

"Did you miss me?" I wondered, chastising myself for acting like a spoiled little high schooler with a crush.

He paused, not entirely sure what I felt. "Will the real Angela please show up?" he joked, tapping me on the forehead. I swatted his hand away and tried to get out of his hold. He only tightened his grip and kissed my cheek to calm me down.

"You're not funny."

"Okay, sorry, baby. I did miss you, and I'm glad you surprised me. I'm slammed with work and back-to-back meetings though. Can we do something together later in the week? Maybe have Granny watch the girls, and we can do dinner and a movie together?" he suggested.

Wanting to ask about the weird smell in his office, yet not wanting to start an unnecessary argument, I agreed and stepped out of his reach. Picking up the food, I started to leave the office.

"Wait... I thought the food was for me?" Brent called out.

"It was for us. Since you're busy and can't step away for lunch, I'm going to have a date with my other man," I taunted with a wink and swaying my hips, giving him something to think about.

"Angela, don't get your ass spanked now!" Brent yelled, and I threw up the middle finger.

* * *

I parked my car in my designated spot in front of my salon and grabbed the bag of food, then headed inside. The salon was packed—just the way I liked it—and I couldn't wait to expand with a second location. The updated white-and-gold interior of the seats, chairs, and sink bowls all matched. Because of the chemicals, the child play area I created was blocked off, so they weren't directly within our sight. It was another extension of the building when I knocked through the wall of the old chicken shack that closed. The second location I dreamed about would be at least two stories with a barbershop included. I would sell my own natural products—and hopefully, my cousins would help run the place.

"Hey, Angela, your next appointment is here—and she's some big-time model, I guess. Kept saying how she only wanted you to do her hair," Kendra, my hair stylist, told me.

I passed the food over to my secretary, walked further into my personal room, and stopped in my tracks when I saw Elena sitting in my chair.

"What the hell are you doing in my chair?" I questioned, sniffing the air and smelling the same perfume. *This tramp was in his office today.*

"I want you to leave Brent alone. In exchange, I'll bring a lot of press and media to your little shop," Elena said, motioning around the room.

I closed my eyes and counted to ten. I needed to breathe and stay calm. The last thing I wanted was to end up in jail behind some little toothpick, baldheaded, no-edge-having model. "Elvira, listen."

"Elena."

"What?"

"My name is Elena, and you know it, among other things you know belong to me."

"Are you high? Because only an idiot high on molly would show up at someone's place of business, without any backup. Brent has proven time and time again: He. Don't. Want. You. Boo," I said, clapping my hands at each word.

"That's a lie—and how does my pussy taste? Since I know you just left him," Elena said with a smirk on her face and her legs crossed.

"You were in his office today?" I inquired. I knew she was telling the truth, and my heart beat fast.

"Yep, surprised he didn't tell you or the other woman. She's your friend, right?"

Emery had looked pissed off earlier that day, and I'd wanted to know why. Now, after getting confirmation from Evillena, I knew the reason my bestie wanted to kick my man's ass. I refused to let her see me falter. At the end of the day, I was the woman he'd decided to be with, and we had two kids at home. He *would* be hearing from me, but this bitch wasn't getting the last word. "You know what, Erica? I think it's time for you to go. Brent made it very clear that he doesn't want you. Find someone else who can clean out that dried-up well you call a pussy and leave my family alone. Otherwise, the old Angela will show up. And honey, she's not as respectful as the new model who has two little girls looking up to her to be a positive role model. Sweetie, you don't want it with me," I explained politely with a smile.

Elena must have felt my last words because she stood, ran her hand down her dress, grabbed her jacket and purse off the couch, and passed by me to the door, trying to avoid knocking me in the shoulder.

I walked back out into the front and told Kimberly to send the next person into my room. I walked to the bathroom to clear my thoughts.

"You will not lose. You will not lose," I kept repeating in front of the mirror, reminding myself to not lose focus. If Brent was serious about being with her, he needed to let me know now. Once I arrived home, I would have a long discussion with him about where this relationship was heading. I refused to play second fiddle to any woman in his life—unless it was our girls.

The rustling of the blow dryer and the raucous laughter in the salon reminded me why I did this. Hearing the latest gossip and seeing the kids on the monitor in the other room, playing and having fun, brightened up my attitude. I finished off the night with three new clients from referrals and gathered more business contacts.

I was planning to do an event to help the female victims of domestic violence down at Granny's church, trying to build confidence with new hair, nails, and facials. Some were going into the workforce for the first time, and that seemed like a good opportunity to not only give back to the community, but also to go to church, so Granny could stop harassing me about Jesus not seeing me in the front pew on Sundays. Arriving home, I cleaned up the toys in the living room and showered. Through the baby monitor, I saw my babies sleeping like angels in their cribs. This was a fantasy I could see and feel.

Chapter Eighteen

Brent

Listening to her light snores, my gaze slowly and seductively slid downward at her plump, round ass under the covers. The weight from the twins had gone straight to her ass, and I was a grateful man. I lifted her leg and gently pushed my way into her warm, tight walls as she lay on her side.

She gasped under her breath. "Baby, Brent, yes... shit!"

I kissed across her shoulder and cheek. She'd come home late last night, and I was already in bed asleep. Elena constantly called my phone, and I ended up turning it off. Angela and I didn't get a chance to catch up with each other like we normally did after work, and I figured this was the best way to wake her up. Then I could fix breakfast before we each went our separate ways.

I groaned in a mixture of pleasure and pain from her tight pussy holding my dick hostage. Biting my lip, I squeezed my eyes shut to calm my thoughts before I released too early. I reached over and gripped her breasts, massaging them with my thumb and speeding up my strokes. I groaned aloud, turning her over onto her stomach and lifting her up with her ass in the air, arching her back. The intensity of our lovemaking was partly me showing her that she was the only woman I wanted, and partly because I could never go a day without being inside her sweet core. When I came, I collapsed forward, and we fell on top of the mattress, breathing heavily.

"Damn, that pussy is lethal, baby."

"Huh," Angela said and snored. Had she just fallen asleep after sex?

I nudged her on the arm. "Baby, are you asleep?" I asked again.

"Baby, give me another hour. I'm tired," Angela mumbled under her breath.

"Are you serious, Angela? Who goes to sleep after some fire-ass sex?" I shouted, not caring if she was disturbed. I was offended when she fell right back to sleep. Not letting it go, I snatched the covers off her naked body and smacked her ass. She jumped up with her hair all over her head and her hands up in a boxing stance. I busted out in laughter at the mean mug she had on her face. I could still see the crustiness in her eyes, but her pussy smelled like sweet peaches—even with the stench of sex in the room.

Surrendering with my hands up to let her know I was sorry, she pushed my hands away, stomped out of the bedroom, and walked toward the bathroom.

"That's not funny, Brent! You're such an asshole, I swear!" she yelled, taking a piss in the toilet with the door open. I shook my head because she was always too comfortable with leaving the bathroom door open, talking about whatever. "We're as one, so that means no secrets."

We negotiated keeping the door closed when it came to doing number two as long as I didn't cut my toenails in bed, something she hated that I did. But keeping the door open during those private movements didn't matter to her. My baby was so backwards.

Finally, Angela emerged after taking care of her morning hygiene routine and ran to get back in bed. I shook my head, walked into the bathroom, and did the same thing. A few minutes later, I came out and looked at her, curled up in bed with drool falling down her face. This was the woman I planned to spend the rest of my life with.

"Baby, move in with me. You and the girls," I asked, walking further to the bed, kissing her all over her face, and biting her bottom lip to wake her back up.

"I like my house, Brent," Angela replied, sliding one eye open and sitting up against the headboard. I sat in front of her and held her hand.

"We can still keep your house for when family comes into town or something, but I want you and my kids with me at all times. I want to wake up to you snoring, the girls crying, and you shitting without thinking of someone walking through the door. I always need your crazy ass next to me, baby. I love your independence and appreciate how you raise our girls to never depend on a man, but we have a family now. Soon, that comes with marriage. We can't live in two separate houses as a married couple," I answered.

"Why not, all the famous celebrities do it?"

"Angie, I'm not asking. You're moving in today, and that's the end of the discussion."

"What about Eloise? Can we discuss that?" Angela spat, rejecting my hand and climbing out of bed.

I blew out a breath of frustration. I knew it was only a matter of time before she came up again. "Who is Eloise, baby?" I remarked, curious if she'd let it go if I just played stupid.

She grabbed her robe out of her walk-in closet. I made a note to myself to have my contractor turn one of my guest rooms into a walk-in closet for her, too. Her nostrils flared with fury. Suddenly, a shoe whizzed past my head, and I ducked on instinct. It was one of my Timberland boots.

"Brent, don't play stupid with me. I told you from the jump—if she was going to be a problem for us, then you had better get it taken care of fast. How do you expect me to move in with you when your sex buddy shows up at my salon after fucking you in your office?"

I was aback by her statement. Thinking over the events of yesterday, Elena was escorted out of my office, and I had my suspicions she'd do something stupid. Going to Angela's shop wasn't something I expected her to do, since I knew Angela came home and didn't call me from jail last night.

"She lied, baby. I didn't sleep with that woman. Yes, she showed up without me knowing and tried to make a pass at me with sex, but Emery showed up and cut her off before anything happened," I answered calmly.

"So, what you're saying is that if Emery didn't show up, you would have slept with her? Is that what I'm hearing?" Angela questioned, throwing the words back at me like stones. Her eyes conveyed the fury simmering within her. Taking a page from Emery and Jackson's book, I wanted to be honest, so we wouldn't have the same problems again in the future, or have her go missing on me with my girls.

"Princess, I'd never stick what belongs to you in any other woman. You have a lock on my heart, mind, and soul. She could never compare to you. Yes, at one point, I was thinking about a future with another woman during our breakup. Once we reconnected, this was it for me, babe. You have to know I would never betray you. Besides, I know Granny gave you a new gun, and I'm not trying to die over a girl who can't hold a candle to you," I said, gathering her into my arms. I held her snugly, caressing her cheek. Her stiffness seemed to fade away, and she allowed me to hold her in my arms. My hands explored the hollows of her back.

"Moving into your house is fine." She relaxed, sinking into my encapsulating embrace.

"Our house," I responded, my lips brushing against hers as I spoke.

"Our house. But what about the Elena situation?" she answered, putting her arms around my neck, straddling my lap and nuzzling her face in my neck.

"Don't worry about her. I'll take care of it. I can't wait to change your last name to Mrs. Townsend," I mused, kissing the pulsing hollow at the base of her throat.

"Me neither, baby, but don't think you're distracting me because I'm still mad at you. Let me get dressed because I'm taking the girls over to hang with Granny and Pops, since most of my appointments are cancelled for today."

"Babe, you know I'm smooth with my charm. How do you think I caught you back in college?" I inquired, waiting for her answer.

"No comment."

She turned sassily, walked around me, and headed to the bathroom. A second later, the door opened, and she was naked, pointing her index finger to join her in the shower.

* * *

I dunked the ball in the net, rebounded, and passed to Jackson. Rather than go into the office on a Friday, I called my boys to have a game and catch up. Damon had been out of town on and off for the last few months, and Jackson was more and more focused on Emery and the kids. He'd become the family man of the group, somewhat a stay-at-home dad, since his business ran itself. Don't get me wrong, I was doing big things in the marketing world and opened a second office in LA. But I wasn't anywhere near the billionaire range like him.

"Yo, man, get the ball! What are you daydreaming about? Angela ain't holding you by the nuts anymore, my guy. You can relax now," Tony, a friend of the group, joked.

I put the middle finger up at him and played defense, covering as Jackson took the ball to the three-point line. Jackson and I were on one team, against Tony and Damon on the other. The games consisted of a hundred-dollar bet each time, and the loser would buy lunch.

"Haha, coming from the guy who has no girl. Only way to get anybody to play with your balls is using your left hand," I retorted, and all the guys chortled.

"My guy thinks he's funny. Tell us, B—when did you last apologize for fucking up with Angela?" Tony said, dribbling the ball from left to right.

"None of your business," I answered, scratching the back of my neck and reminiscing on the events of this morning.

"See dude scratch his neck, it was today I bet. Come on, tell us." Tony and Damon burst into laughter.

"Man, just shoot the ball or forfeit the game."

"Aw, is he getting ready to cry now? My guy, it's all good. We've all been there with the ladies."

"How the hell are you going to come at me when you're still single at forty years old. Man, please, at least I got a woman and kids waiting at home for me."

"Yep, because you want that family life. I'm good, player, riding the waves and getting a nut from all the beautiful women without the headache of a relationship," Tony explained, still dribbling the ball.

"So, you think at forty, that's something to brag about?" I replied, gestured to the ball, and stole it, crossing over Damon and taking it to the rim.

"Listen, women need two types of guys in this world. They have the committed guy and the fun guy. I happen to fall under the fun guy. I give them multiple orgasms, and you gentlemen happen to be the family guys who pay their bills and take care of the kids so they can go shopping and then hang with guys like me," he said nonchalantly and shrugged his shoulders. We all jerked back at his statement.

"Motherfucker, if you don't get your five-foot-six, Chris-Brown-reject-looking, momma-boy ass somewhere and pass the ball..." I joked and ran the ball down the court.

Everybody laughed at my dig, and he threw his middle finger up at me. "Yeah, this Chris Brown motherfucker can still get yo woman with his big..." he tried to say, and I charged at him, but Damon and Jackson held me back. He started laughing behind Damon, holding his arms up in mock surrender.

"You know you're wrong for speaking on his girl, man," Damon spoke with a thoughtful frown, pulling his eyebrows together.

"Don't test me, Tony!" I remarked, not a vestige of humor showing on my face.

I slapped hands with Jackson and Damon, shaking my head, annoyed. I ignored Tony and walked off toward the benches to grab my gym bag and check my messages. Seeing nothing that required my immediate attention back at the office, I headed home to wait for my girl with a little surprise.

* * *

I'd finally put the last box of Angela's things in our place even though she'd say it was my place. I honestly didn't care if it was my place or hers even though I had the bigger home. Having these moments of us together as a family under one roof made it all worth the fights and long-distance talks.

"What are you doing just standing there?" Angela barked, holding Marcia in her arms. I noticed she had a bit of spit up on her shoulder. I thought she never looked more gorgeous.

I chortled, shaking my head. Both my babies looked exhausted.

"Give me my baby before you drive her crazy."

"Please, your baby is driving me crazy. I think she has a fever or is getting back at me for something."

I wiped Marcia's mouth and kissed her cheek, sitting her on the couch and rubbing her back as she yawned, rubbing her sleepy eyes.

"And why is she getting back at you, Angela?" I said,

wondering how a baby could get revenge on a grown woman.

"For one, you have them both spoiled, and I think we kept them up the other night with our little interlude."

"Girl, ain't nothing little over here. You mean our sex?"

"Shush. Don't say the s word around my babies," Angela snapped, covering Marcia's ears like she could understand us.

"You're tripping, woman. What are we having for dinner?" I picked up the remote as Angela curled up next to me on the couch. I pulled her under my arms, kissing her forehead.

"This is nice."

"I know, and just think we have many more years of this to look forward to."

"Ugh... Well, in that case, I'll need a bigger closet and my own bank account for my shoes."

"What's wrong with the closets?"

"Have you not seen the closets that the Real House-wives have? Boy, you're rich, and I'm not settling with my half of a walk-in."

We both burst out in laughter and watched the latest episode of Iyanna: Fix My Life.

Chapter Nineteen

Angela

Pops sat contentedly in his chair with Jazmine, who was trying to bite his finger and giggling. Seeing this visual of my family was special to me. Marcia was strapped onto Granny's chest while she cooked lunch for us. I'd worked so much this past week and wanted to make sure I kept my promise to let the girls hang with their grandparents. Pushing my annoyance at Elena out of my mind, I decided to let Brent handle it. If I didn't, I knew I'd end up with a murder charge. But I figured that Jackson had friends in high places and could get me off if I pleaded insanity because I went crazy over someone harassing my family.

"Angela, pass me the salt out of the cabinet," Granny called out as she turned the burner down on the stove and opened the fridge, grabbing a bottle for Marcia.

"Aren't you supposed to cut back on salt?

"When did you get a degree in medicine, little girl?

She cooed at Marcia as she took the bottle into her mouth. My baby was so greedy and spoiled, no one could tell her anything.

"When the doctor told you to cut back, and might I add, all the heavy meals you like to cook aren't helping.

"Doctor said it's all about moderation. If I'm not mistaken, you've never complained about my meals before? So cut the bull and tell me what's going on in your world. I've talked with Emery and Jordan this past week but not you.

"Okay, old lady."

"This old lady can still whip your ass. Now, catch me up on what's going on while I feed my baby. She's looking more and more like you every day."

"Besides hanging with my babies, Brent and I are fine. We're talking, and I moved in with him finally. We're trying to make this whole family thing work, and his old girlfriend is trying to sabotage things. You remember Elena the model?"

Granny took Marcia out of her straps and placed her in the playpen next to the table, so we could watch her as we ate. She picked up a plate and scooped a nice amount of shrimp, spaghetti, garlic bread, and chitterlings onto it. I hated chitterlings and always passed on them whenever she cooked them, but it was Pops' favorite dish, and she made sure her man was spoiled.

"Here, let me take a plate to my husband," she stated and passed my plate over. I poured lemonade into my glass as she walked off. A few minutes later, she walked back inside with Jazmine and laid her down in the playpen with her sister. She then fixed herself a plate. "What did Brent say about her? I *know* you're not jealous." Granny sat across from me after fixing her own plate and picked a napkin up to place over her lap. Grabbing her fork, she dove into her meal and quietly looked at me.

"He had another one of his excuses, and then I caught

him in a lie and broke up with him, but that only lasted for a minute in my mind before he told me she doesn't mean anything to him and to focus on our family. Can I be honest?" A sigh caught in my throat.

"I tell you all the time you can be honest with me. I know you better than anyone, Angela."

"A part of me feels guilty because he wanted to get married a few years back, and I turned him down, so we broke up. I wanted to do my own thing and date different guys. Seeing him with other women always pissed me off, and I thought if we somehow got back together, I would forgive him if he cheated because I wasn't the best person as a girlfriend back then. Now, after seeing Elena and the things she's doing to get his attention, if he slips up, I don't know if I could easily look the other way—even though I have no room to talk."

"Brent wouldn't cheat on you, Angela. Yes, you're more than difficult to deal with, and I can attest to that."

"Tell me how you really feel then," I mumbled under my breath.

"If I can't be honest with you for a minute, baby, the outside world will. Judging you is the last thing I'm doing, honey. You don't know this, and I tried to keep my relationship with Pops something you girls could look up to, but in our younger years though, we hurt each other and learned from those mistakes. Brent loves you, and I know seeing him move on was hard, but you needed to grow up. No, you're not your mother and father's relationship, and they weren't happy together. You have to let that hurt go, because he won't abandon what you've built. Being a mother and wife is another gift that God has placed in your life. Running from it in the beginning, I understood, because you needed to forgive and learn to grow up. But allowing a person to question the commitment he's given you and showed you is something I won't tolerate."

"What do you mean about allow?"

"Allowing Elena to have one section in your brain to question Brent's loyalty to you is letting her win. I'm the first one who would ride out with you to kill a bitch if she fucks with my money, man, or family. Don't allow your headspace to get cluttered with her presence, baby."

"When did you become this hardcore gangster, Granny?"

"Sweetie, before I was Granny, I was Lynn. Don't let the age on my driver's license fool you."

"You think he wants to get married? I know his last engagement didn't work out, and I refuse to disappoint him because I'm not living up to the standards of what he feels a wife is supposed to be."

"Girl, don't let society tell you what a wife is supposed to do or become. Be you and communicate with him, and the rest will fall into place. There's no one way to be a wife. Back in my day, of course, they wanted you barefoot in the kitchen and pregnant while the man worked, but we made our own rules, and I chose to stay home. Look at Emery and Jordan; they both work and have families. Are you thinking of staying home?"

"Nope, and I'm planning to open another salon. Brent slowed down on his traveling so things at the office are fine, and he's hiring more people to help take the workload off him."

She stood and grabbed my plate, taking it to the sink as I looked in on the girls sleeping. They both cuddled up close to each other with Marcia holding Jazmine's hand. I brushed a hand across her cheek and walked to the counter to help her with the dishes.

"Then stop worrying about something that hasn't happened. When he pops the question, let him know what your expectations are and discuss things like an adult," she explained. Thinking over her words, I realized she was right once again. Communication is the key to any type of relationship and being upfront with what I needed and expected was the first step in whatever direction we went from here on out.

* * *

One week later, I was in the car with my best friends, checking my lipstick and hair. Brent was supposed to take me out, but then he canceled at the last minute. So, they called me to hang out, since we hadn't talked in a while. We'd arranged plans for dinner—a girls' night without the men. Emery was celebrating signing another client, I'd booked a hair show, and Jordan was coming back from a mini vacation with her man. So, we had a lot of catching up to do before our busy lives took over again.

Emery was driving, I was in the passenger side, and Jordan was in the back on her phone, texting nonstop.

"Jordan, tell Damon you are fine and get off that phone, damn. We said no contact with our men tonight," I spat, popping my lips emphatically to make sure the lipstick was evenly layered.

"Stop being a hater."

"Leave her alone, Angela. I'm surprised Brent let you out of the house dressed like that."

"As far as I know, Brent ain't my daddy, and I'm grown, so he can't tell me what to wear, unlike your man Jackson," I chortled, pointing my finger at Emery wearing a long black dress with long sleeves and a side split.

"Jackson happens to like the way I dress, and I picked this out myself," she commented haughtily, rolling her eyes.

I shrugged and put my mirror back in my purse, then looked out the window. We'd been driving for the past fifteen minutes, and I was starving.

"How is everything at the salon and the girls?" Emery inquired as she turned into the restaurant parking lot.

"Things at the salon are fine; we can talk about that when I've had a couple of drinks and can let loose. My girls are getting big and are spoiled incessantly by the family—especially their daddy and uncles," I replied, unlocking my seatbelt and grabbing my purse. I let the valet open my door and stepped out, smoothing my dress down. As I walked toward the door, someone almost side-swiped another car to get a parking space, and I cursed them out. Emery yanked me by the arm and shook her head at me as we walked inside.

Chapter Twenty

Brent

She was determined to drive me crazy with trying to do this parenting thing alone. We often clashed on the little things, but her good intentions over the years of forcing me away, brought us together.

Standing here at dinner waiting impatiently for her arrival, our entire family gathered around the table knowing I was popping the question tonight.

I knew she felt I was pulling away and being distant. It was just a part of my plan to get her here tonight and finally make her see that I wasn't that person from college anymore. It was time for us both to grow up and become a family.

As the doors opened, I heard her before I even saw her. She was complaining about someone's parking. I chuckled, turned around, and met her gaze. She stood alongside Jordan and Emery. She wore her hair in one of those goddess braids or some shit. She was wearing light makeup, and the diamond earrings I'd bought her when I came back from LA.

She wore a baby-blue, floral-print lace dress. Her gaze

trailed over me as I stood in my dark-blue suit and tie with the gold cufflinks she'd purchased for me for my birthday last year. Even though we were separated, she somehow made her presence known. I had to hold my hands in front of me, trying to will my growing erection to calm down before I had to take her into the bathroom and end our night before it even began. I slowly walked over to her and reached for her hand to pull her into the middle of the crowd. Granny, Pops, Emery's parents, my parents, and Angela's cousins all stood around, cheering. I slowly bent down on one knee as her hands covered her mouth in shock. A tear fell down her cheek.

"Surprise!" everyone yelled at the same time and brought out their cameras to film the moment.

"Brent..." she whispered in shock, and I raised her hand to kiss her palm.

"Angela, as I stand here with you in front of our family and friends, I often look back on our relationship and think, 'Why did I ever ask her out?'" I joked, and everyone laughed.

She tried to release her hand from mine, and I only tightened my hold. "You know why you stayed. Don't act like a clown in front of company and our children," Angela spat.

A part of me reveled in open admiration of this strong woman who dealt with so much pain, to come full circle and let me love her and make her my wife.

"Angela, I love you, and we both know the road we've traveled wasn't easy. We didn't have the best blueprint for making this relationship work. The one thing I can promise you is that I'll always be there during the good and bad times. Would you do me the honor of being my wife?" I pulled a small black box out of my pocket and opened it. Everyone in the room gasped in awe. I'd spared no expense in purchasing a custom-made diamond ring with her initials and our kids' initials engraved inside.

Her features became more animated as I held up the ring. She fanned herself, willing her tears to stop, as Jordan and Emery both passed her tissues. "You sure about this, B?" Angela's body seemed to vibrate with new life, even as her eyes narrowed in suspicion.

"Baby, you're the only one for me. Forget about the past and focus on our future. I'm serious about us being a family with our girls. Then you can give me another set, possibly triplets, after the girls turn one."

"Boy, are you crazy? I'm not having triplets. Let alone any more kids. What do I look like, popping out more babies without a ring? Wait a minute, is this why you're proposing?"

"What? Of course not!" I answered and stared into her eyes, baffled by her question. If anything, I would have married her after college, before we both drifted toward our careers.

"Granny, what do you think?" Angela asked, peering over my shoulder at Granny, who was hugging Pops' arm.

She nodded with a resounding, "Yes," as tears poured from her eyes.

Angela lowered her gaze and ran a hand across my cheek and lifted my chin. "Yes, Brent! I'll marry you. Can I still call you my baby daddy though?"

"Hell no!" everyone in the room yelled.

I slid the ring on her finger, took her palm, and stood, wrapping my arms around her waist and closing the gap between us. She put her arms around my neck, and I leaned down to kiss her lips as she raised herself to meet mine. I placed a slow, lingering kiss on her lips in remembrance of our first kiss back in college. This was the anniversary of our first date. She succumbed to the forceful domination of my lips, just as Emery and Jordan stepped in to pull us apart before things could heat up.

"Okay, you two, we have children and elderly people here. Save that for when you get home."

"Mm-hmm, she's right, babe. We have all night to celebrate."

Angela wiped the remnants of her red lipstick on my face and bit her lip to stifle a grin.

"Jordan, can you watch the girls tonight?" Angela asked and looked at me with amused wonder illuminating her face.

Her eyes were filled with a curious, deep longing. I wanted to show her what the next fifty years of our lives would look like once we said I do. Even at the club and hanging with our friends, I only felt her presence, and no other woman could ever come close to how she made me feel. So, tonight, I'd make it all about her—the woman I loved, the mother of my children, and the friend and partner I always needed by my side.

* * *

Even though we had a big dinner celebration with family and friends around, I wanted our personal space to be filled with only us. At the house earlier, I spoke with Emery and Jordan to help me plan the surprise celebration. I commissioned Emery and Jordan to setup champagne, start a bubble bath, and decorate with photos of our middle school years, all the way up to the birth of our kids. Peering at the photos and knowing how we'd come full circle stirred an ache in my chest. We missed out on so many years because of our miscommunication and stubbornness. I was a fool, and she was selfish at times, so to see her in our home, wearing only a thong and the engagement ring on her finger, put everything into perspective as we navigated the next steps in our relationship.

I bent down and pecked her plump, swollen lips. We'd already made out in the taxi on our way back and hearing Angela's loud moans had me at the point of wanting to rip her dress off right there in the back of the cab.

"What are you thinking about?" Angela asked, as she leaned up to unbuckle my belt. I unbuttoned my dress shirt, looking her over seductively, and kissed her awaiting mouth. She pulled me in close. A sense of urgency drove her to flip me over and straddle my lap.

"I see someone is anxious."

She leaned over and ran a hand across my cheek, slowly caressing as my hands moved up and down her thighs and hips, and then up to squeeze her breasts. After the birth of our girls, I noticed she went up a cup size. Plus, her ass was already big, but now, after the birth of our babies, her two round cheeks looked like the perfect set of peaches that I loved devouring.

"Fuck me until I can't come anymore. Can you do that?" she whispered and licked from the bottom of my ear to the top.

I flipped us over again, and she lay against my body, chest to chest. Her breathing picked up as my tongue traced every angle of her shoulder, down to her perfect, plump breasts with the stretch marks that I loved. She and the other girls often cried and fussed about the extra weight and stretch marks. As her man, I reminded her that she gave birth to our kids, and it was a part of womanhood. It didn't make her less attractive to me; instead, it made me more turned on to know her body was natural and beautiful.

"Mrs. Townsend, it would be my pleasure."

Her gaze roved from my lips, down to my dick outline, standing at attention in my boxers.

"Take him out."

Angela bit her bottom lip as I reached over and gripped her left breast gently. I squeezed and teased her nipple, feeling the heat emanating from her covered mound, wanting desperately to be inside her. We both had a huge appetite for oral sex, but I needed to taste every divine inch of her body.

"You taste so good, baby," I mumbled, letting go of her left breast and moving to her right one as she held a tight grip on my dick.

"I love you, Brent," Angela replied and wrapped her leg around my right hip, pushing me in closer to stop the longing and separation of our bodies. She rested a hand on my hip with her nails digging in deeper as I twisted and kneaded her right nipple.

"Please don't keep me waiting."

Warmth spread across my chest at her begging and pleading. I winked and moved down, taking my right and left index finger and pulling her thong down and tossing it to the floor. Taking her right foot in my hand, I kissed the palm of her foot, massaging the way she liked from the ball of her ankle all the way up to the pinky toes.

"Yes, Brent."

A smile parted my lips as she let go and gave in to the pleasure I was planning to give us both. I trailed kisses down her leg to her inner thigh, and then teased her with one finger, entering her sweet pussy. She gripped my shoulders and shuddered under my hold. A grin creased my face as I went deeper and teased her with my tongue. Her tempting moans and stifled movements caused the corner of my lip to tug up in an inviting smile. She opened her eyes and stared down at me.

"How is this, Mrs. Townsend?" I teased, placing a gentle kiss on her inner thigh.

"Brent, you drive me crazy. I swear if you ever cheat on me or leave, I promise to drive to your momma's house and beat her ass," Angela told me, completely out of breath.

I smacked her inner thigh and slid up to align my dick with her warm, tight pussy. I entered her slowly, teasing with just the tip.

"Shit, why are you always threatening me, woman?" I kissed her cheek and pushed in further.

"Ahhh, damn it, because I've loved you for so long, and the thought of anyone else getting the best of you kills me. Knowing that your parents created a beautiful man who loves my craziness. I wouldn't be able to move on if you ever left me," Angela spoke as our mouths connected, and I slid my tongue inside, gripped her by the waist as I thrust faster. The bed rocked, and the headboard banged. Glad we didn't have the kids tonight.

"Oh, God, baby! Yes!"

"You feel that? Huh, Angie, answer me, baby." I ran a hand over her stomach, up her chest, feeling her heart thrumming underneath my palm. I ran a hand around her neck, gently squeezed, and lifted her leg over my shoulder, falling deeper into her core.

"You never have to worry about another woman. This pussy is all I need, baby. Damn, I need another taste," I said and pulled out abruptly as her juices ran down her thigh and my dick, onto the sheets. She shivered as sweat beads drizzled down her chest and stomach.

She opened her legs wider, and I found my happy place once again and ate her from top to bottom. Angela gripped my head, holding me in place. She thrust into my mouth, feeding me her sweet juices. In and out, my tongue went, fast and sharp, applying pressure on her clit. She screamed as her orgasm finally crested over her.

"I can't feel my legs, baby. What the fuck?" Angela moaned in pleasure. I smacked her on the ass, to turn around and arch her back.

"That's good loving, baby. Once you take my last name, you'll have plenty of nights with that same feeling. Get used to it now and don't act surprised when I want it three times a day," I joked, and she tried to push me away from her. We both laughed, and I kissed both her ass cheeks and rubbed a hand up and down her back.

My dick eased back inside, and we both shuddered in comfort at the blissful feeling of our bodies being intertwined together.

"I love you," Angela moaned and gripped the sheets with one hand and the headboard with the other.

For the rest of the night, we changed positions and climaxed together, screaming I love you and promising to make our relationship a priority, so we wouldn't fall into the same trap as her parents.

We fell asleep in each other's arms, contemplating our lives together. Our time apart not only made us both grow and mature, but it also gave us a sense of perspective on what we wanted out of each other. It made us realize that our individual selves could still focus on our goals and dreams and not feel pressured to choose.

Chapter Twenty-One

Jordan

The next day after the engagement party, we went over to the club to continue the celebration. Emery's parents took all the kids, and Granny spent the night over there. Pops was upset at first, and said, I quote, "My woman sleeps next to me." We all laughed at Granny, rolling her eyes at him. Eventually, he caved and went with her, since all six kids would be in one place. I didn't drink, since I was pregnant again, and no one knew yet. So far, hiding the signs wasn't bad since I was in the early stages at four weeks.

Angela brought her hand up to stifle her giggles as Emery recreated his attitude from the engagement dinner.

"Jordan, you remember, Granny said this was the first time that Angela was ever speechless in her life."

I nodded, peeling off a piece of bread as we sat at Ruth's Diner, having lunch outside. Angela had canceled her appointments; Emery had moved her meeting to tomorrow, and I was currently on leave from teaching. Having three kids at home and a husband was a lot, and sometimes overwhelming. I understood why Angela wanted to wait before having more kids. At first, I was working part-time before the baby was born, then afterwards, Damon was traveling more with his agency, and he wanted us all together, so I stepped back to focus on making new memories in our new home that we'd bought together.

"Yeah, and it's all because she's finally getting married and becoming someone's wife."

"I'm still a little hungover from last night. My man wore me out and then wanted to have a quickie in the shower before I left to come here," Angela said, taking a sip of her water and adjusting her shades.

"I bet your ass gave him some, didn't you?" Emery teased and motioned her hands together, mimicking giving oral sex.

"Oh, trap, I'm not the one on my third child," Angela said and peered over at me.

"What?" I questioned innocently.

"Jordan, we're your best friends; we can tell you're knocked up. Your face is fuller; you've been home more and not hanging out; you stopped drinking on our girls' nights—and sis, your ass has never been that big unless you're pregnant," Angela replied and pointed at me as the waitress brought our food over.

"Thank God you said something. I was trying to be patient and wait for her to tell us. I can't believe another little baby is coming," Emery stated and clapped her hands, cheering over the news.

"I was planning on telling you guys after I talk with Damon and my parents."

"Well, keep that same attitude when you tell Granny and your parents. You know how that old lady gets when we keep secrets," Angela said, cutting into her omelet and taking a bite. She loved breakfast no matter the time of day, or what restaurant we were at. She loved ordering breakfast. On her plate was a salmon omelet, fruit on the side, crispy potatoes, and French toast. I only had a salad and water. While Emery ordered coffee, waffles, scrambled eggs, and ham.

"So, what are we going to do about this wedding?" Emery asked, changing the subject.

"I didn't tell Brent, but I want something simple. Just us at the courthouse and a dinner at the house," Angela answered right as a tall woman who looked familiar stood with her arms across her chest. She gave us a hostile glare, and I wasn't the fighting type of person, especially since I was pregnant again.

"Can we help you, Eloise?" Angela sputtered, bristling with indignation.

"It's Elena, and you know it, *Angelica*," Elena spat, rolling her eyes in annoyance as her two friends looked on and giggled.

"Bitch! Be happy I even addressed you," Angela said in anger.

Emery and I both looked on in shock, trying to assess the situation. Elena slapped her hand down on the table, and Angela tried to get up, but Emery pushed her back down by the shoulder.

"Listen, Elena, I don't know or care what the situation is, but please leave. We're having a private conversation."

Elena brushed me off with a wave as Angela shook with impotent rage. "Brent is my man, and you need to back off. We were happy before you came along and seduced him into thinking those snot-nosed kids belong to him." Elena chuckled and high-fived her friend.

Angela was quiet—*too* quiet—and that only meant she was out for blood, and no one could stop her—not even Granny and Pops. Emery quickly pulled the knives off the table, and I grabbed her plate on the other end, so nothing could be thrown.

"What did you just say?" Angela inquired calmly.

"I said Brent was, and is, happy with me. I suggest you find someone else to trick into being your baby daddy because he doesn't love you, sweetie," Elena stated, flinging the words at her like stones.

The waitress walked over because of the commotion and asked if everything was all right. Angela laughed and slowly stood. I could tell she was embarrassed at the idea of Brent thinking he wasn't the father of her two kids. Suddenly, Angela stood and punched Elena solidly in the nose, taking a handful of her hair and slinging her onto the ground. She straddled her and continued to rain down blows at her face.

The manager and security came over, trying to break them up as Elena screamed in pain to get her away and call the police.

"Angela, stop! You're going to kill her!" I yelled, trying to help Emery pull the manager off Angela. Her two friends tried to jump into the fray and help, but Emery pulled out her taser. I guess all those nights of Granny teaching us all self-defense had finally paid off.

"Every time I see you, I'm whipping your ass. Don't you *ever* in your miserable life talk about my kids, you nasty slut," Angela growled and shoved Elena in the head. Her clothes and hair were completely out of place, and her nose was bleeding.

"I want her arrested. She belongs in jail like the rest of the savages," Elena said with a smirk on her face.

"You set me up, didn't you? Let me go!" Angela yelled as the police came inside, and the manager pulled her toward them. Emery and I followed, trying to defuse the situation.

"What's the problem?" the officer asked.

"She started a fight in my place of business. I want her arrested and banned from here." The manager glowered at us and turned away to help Elena.

"That bitch came over and started with us," Angela explained.

"You can plead your case down at the station," the officer stated, taking his handcuffs out of his belt as Emery pulled her phone out to make a call.

"What are you arresting her for? She was only defending herself?" I said, moving between the front door, trying to stop them from leaving.

"Ma'am, I suggest you get out of the way, unless you want to end up like your friend here." The officer gripped Angela's arm tighter as she tried to kick Elena as they walked toward us at the exit.

"Officer, I will be pressing charges immediately. This woman has been harassing me and my man for months now. Showing up at his work unannounced, Claiming he has children by her. You do realize who I am, correct?" Elena explained as her whole demeanor shifted to an evil, conniving, little bitch, one who knew exactly how to manipulate others to get what she wanted.

"Elena, why are you lying? You've been calling Brent and hanging up. Slashing his tires and showing up at his job. Girl, get a life and find yourself someone else to play with before I shove my foot up your ass," Angela harshly spat, angry with herself for letting someone cause her to act out of character.

"You're mistaken; Brent and I aren't broken up, and we've been very happy these last few months. I'll admit he was curious about your claims, but things seemed to have worked themselves out, and we're having a baby together," Elena taunted and rubbed her stomach, smiling as she walked out of the restaurant. Angela's embarrassment deepened and grew into anger.

"Let her go. She didn't do anything wrong."

The other officer grabbed my elbow and placed me under arrest right as Emery got off the phone.

"I called Brent and Jackson. They'll meet us down at the station," Emery said, following Angela and me out the door.

"Call him back and tell him don't worry about coming down. Jackson can handle getting us out. If not, Granny will, and tell Brent she's keeping my kids until I get out," Angela explained, trying to hide her inner misery and sorrow at having to deal with this situation so soon after her big night.

"Angela."

Angela cut her off with a wave of her hand as the officer placed us both in the backseat of the car. He shut the door, came around to the driver's side, and got in. Emery stood outside with the other officer, getting information about where we would be taken into custody.

"What a way to celebrate my engagement and your pregnancy; we end up in handcuffs. Who would have thought?" Angela chuckled under her breath.

"Brent and Jackson will fix this, and then we can go back to planning your wedding reception," I joked, praying she wasn't serious about ending things with Brent.

"Jordan, I'm not getting married. Did you not just see

what I was dealing with a few minutes ago? That girl has way too many screws loose, and if she keeps playing with me, I'll for-real end up in jail for homicide—especially if she keeps talking about my kids."

"Angela, you can't say things like that in front of a police officer."

We finally pulled off as she shrugged her shoulders and stared out the window.

"I had a feeling this would happen," Angela mumbled under her breath.

"What did you say?"

"Nothing, Jordan, nothing."

"Okay, Angela Jones, seems like you've been a busy girl. I have a warrant for your arrest on outdated traffic tickets. Get comfortable because you'll be with us for a while." The officer chuckled as he drove, turning onto the freeway. The shock of discovery hit her full force as a tear trickled down her face. This wasn't the time to berate her anymore, so I leaned my head on her shoulder in comfort as we pulled into the police station fifteen minutes later.

Soon as the door opened, Emery's car pulled up with Granny inside, plus Jackson and his lawyer. I felt a little relief but at the same time disappointment because Damon was out of town. Once he heard the news, plus that of my pregnancy, I could imagine my days of hanging out would be restricted to our backyard.

"Ladies, move forward. Let's go," the officer said.

"Don't say anything, Angela; keep your mouth shut until the lawyer tells you to speak. Fat ass out here, fighting like she's a teenager with no kids at home. I swear, I have no idea where I went wrong," Granny scolded. Jackson held the door open for her and Emery.

"Granny, don't act like you've never been arrested,"

Angela teased, trying to mask her irritation with the whole situation.

"If I did, I had enough sense to not put my kids in a bad situation where they wouldn't have me around," Granny answered, jabbing her finger against Angela's chest.

"Jordan, I spoke with Damon, and he's catching the first flight back tonight and should be home in a few hours," Jackson stated, wrapping his arm around Emery's shoulders. The lawyer walked back with us to the booking area as Granny, Jackson, and Emery stayed in the front waiting room to hear about posting bail.

Chapter Twenty-Two

Brent

"Elena, I don't care what you think. I'm in love with Angela, and she's going to be my wife. What the hell were you thinking, playing these childish games?" I paced in her living room. She'd called, talking about hurting herself. When I arrived, she was wearing next to nothing. Dread and anger fueled me at the thought of Angela sitting at the jail, thinking about me betraying her trust and getting another woman pregnant—which I knew wasn't true. We always used protection, and the last time we had sex was over four months ago, right before I moved from LA. Yeah, I'd continued seeing her during our little breakup, but I'd stayed celibate because the back and forth pissed me off so much, and my dick only got hard for Angela's crazy ass.

"Brent, you don't mean that, baby. We both know Angela is not right for you." Elena stood and walked toward me to kiss my lips.

I backed up, halting her right when the doorbell rang. "Are you expecting someone?" I asked, stepping to the side as she opened the door with a shocked look on her face. Angela and her cousins stood at her door, smiling.

Granny told me she would be at the police station for a while, and I thought I had plenty of time to talk some sense into Elena to get her to stop harassing us before I put a restraining order out.

"Well, isn't this a small world? Our baby daddy must have decided to sleep with you tonight, thinking I was locked up. Shush, Elena; you're welcome," Angela said, surprisingly calm.

"Angela, baby, it's not what you think. I came to tell her to leave us alone." I tried to reach out for her, and she stepped back, rejecting my hand. Elena looked at her in surprise. The shock caused my words to wedge in my throat; her refusal would put us back to square one. "Angela, think about this before you jump to conclusions. I was at work, and Jackson called me about the arrest earlier. I flew home to get Elena to drop the charges."

"Is that why she's dressed in skimpy shorts and a crop-top spaghetti-strap shirt? What exactly was the leverage to get her to be quiet, Brent? Huh!"

Elena smirked and tried to wrap her arms around me, and I pushed her hands away. Angela turned away and walked off as her cousins leapt forward and jumped on Elena. A part of me felt bad and wanted to break it up but seeing Angela getting in her car and driving off made me want to follow her and make things right before the wedding.

"Brent! Help me please. Stop, I'm sorry. I don't want him," Elena cried out.

Twenty minutes later, I pulled up to our house and sat for a second, getting my thoughts together. Angela had the light on in the living room, and I could see her pacing back and forth. The door was wide open. She peeked out just as I stepped out of the car.

"Hurry up and get your shit before I burn it like Angela Bassett did in *Waiting to Exhale*! Got me having kids for you and wearing your ring! Hmph, you done lost your damn mind! Actually, let me find the gun that Granny got me for my birthday last year and go back over to Miss Elena's house. I'll show her crazy!" Angela shouted, and then walked back into the house. I followed her upstairs, closing the door behind me.

"She's going to make me pay for this for a while."

"You're damn right I am!" Angela yelled, just as I got to the door. *Oops, must have said that part aloud.* She stepped around me, so I wouldn't block her, and she opened the dresser drawers, taking my clothes out.

I stood back and chuckled to myself.

"Are you laughing at me? Is this funny to you?"

"Baby, you and I both know nothing happened with that girl. So, tell me what you're mad about, so I can fix it, and we can get back to our wedding plans."

"Do I have an S tattooed on my forehead?" she asked and walked closer to me.

I shook my head, and she slapped me on my forehead.

"Exactly, you didn't get a stupid bimbo for a girl-friend, Brent. This is one of the reasons I wanted to be single in college. Men are dogs. Now my ass has two kids, I'm trying to run a business, and deal with your drama. I should have never gotten involved with you, Mr. Townsend."

Anger vibrated off my skin at her even thinking she was the only one affected by this tumultuous relationship. The push and pull, and constant tug of war to see who had the upper hand became toxic in college, and I'd hoped she'd grown up.

"We're not doing this, Angela. You're damn near thirty years old and playing the same game as Elena. Before you go off, I'm letting you know this between us is forever. I placed that ring on your finger, and you agreed to be my wife in good times and bad."

"That was before I got arrested over your girlfriend."

"We had broken up before you and I got back together!" I yelled, hitting my chest in frustration.

"I don't care!"

"Baby, I'm not your father or your mother. Yes, they left you with a lot of open wounds, but you've had Emery and her family—plus me—to help you become whole again. Like I said, I'm never leaving you like he left your mom and you. The only person who makes me laugh and drives me crazy with her snoring is you. Plus, my dick doesn't get hard for anyone but you," I answered and pulled her close into my arms.

She tried to fight my tight grip around her waist. I bent down to kiss her lips, and she moved her face out of the way. "She said you told her the kids aren't yours. How could she even know about my children, Brent?" Angela asked and looked up to peer into my eyes as tears streamed down her face.

I lifted her chin and kissed each tear away. "Elena and I only spoke about the kids when you invited me to meet you for lunch after we saw each other at Jordan's party with Damon."

"I don't remember that part," Angela responded, stepped out of my reach, and headed to sit on the bed. She turned away without waiting for a reply, leaned over the bed, and crossed her ankles. Angela sighed and covered her eyes with her arm.

I sat next to her, running a hand over her thigh up to her arm and kissed her lips. Her coolness was evidence that she wasn't amused with the drama from my ex.

"What will make you forget about this day and focus on our wedding?" I tapped her on the ass gently and laid my leg across hers to snuggle in close.

"Umm, if you can ship Elena off to Saudi Arabia, that would be great."

"What! Why Saudi Arabia?"

"Because if I see her in my city again, I'm going to run her over and end up in jail. So, it's best to ship her off somewhere I know she can't be thought of again."

"Baby, you can't always threaten people with violence."

Angela tried to push me off her and sit up. I tightened my grip and kissed the back of her neck.

"Brent, let's be clear. The dick ain't that good. You'd never catch me acting a fool over you, calling and hanging up or stalking you at your job."

"Girl, please. How many times in college did you fake like you were sick, or my mom called with an emergency and needed me, so you'd break up my date? I love you, but the only difference between you and Elena is she doesn't have a gun."

"Quit lying. Anyway, I doubt she'll be a problem for us going forward. This is one of those times I appreciate having cousins younger than me to help fight. Emery and Jordan are too soft now."

"Okay, baby. What took you so long to get out of jail?" I asked, getting out of bed and helping her sit up.

My stomach grumbled, and she snickered, stood, and

pecked my lips. "I had some outstanding parking tickets that I forgot to pay," Angela answered, following me out of the bedroom toward the kitchen.

I shook my head and chuckled at her response. "What's so funny?" Angela inquired, stepping out of my hold to open the fridge.

"We always knew you'd end up in jail, I just didn't think it would be over parking tickets." I laughed aloud. She mocked my laughing and went back to look into the fridge, grabbing a steak and vegetables.

My phone vibrated in my pocket, I pulled it out and saw a message from Emery, checking to see if Angela made it home safe.

Emery: *How is she?*

Me: *She's good, about to eat dinner.*

Emery: *Tell her to call me tomorrow.*

Me: *For sure, and let Jackson know to hit me up later this week.*

"Who is that?" Angela placed the steak on the counter. I walked up behind her and kissed the side of her neck and showed her my phone.

"Emery, just checking in to make sure you made it home safe. You need any help?"

"Tell her I'll call her in the morning. Keep me company while I get the food started."

Me: *She said that she'll call you tomorrow.*

I replied and put my phone back inside my pocket. I focused my attention back on her as she bent over and pulled the skillet out of the bottom cabinet. Watching the infamous Angela Jones turn into a wife, mom, cooking homebody was a remarkable thing to see.

"Are we still on for the wedding?" I asked, staring into her eyes.

The tension was thick, as she placed the knife down and wiped her hands on the dishtowel next to the food. She walked toward me as I sat at the table. Angela bent down and kissed my lips—once, twice—and then straightened up again. "Even though I should leave you alone—since I technically ended up in some drama with your ex—I guess I'll give you the honor of being my husband and not just my baby daddy," Angela said, drawing the hem of her dress up teasingly and showing off her legs.

"Did you think I would let you get away from me that easy? We've been through too much. Our kids wouldn't like me calling someone else Mommy," I teased, and she turned around fast with her knife pointing at me, eyes narrowed in anger.

I raised my hands up in mock surrender. "Too soon?" I asked with a grin.

"Ugh, yeah, asshole," Angela answered.

Two hours later, we lay in bed, talking about our wedding plans and how the family would feel about our elopement.

"The big wedding can come later, when the girls get older, and my second shop is off the ground. Emery and Jordan are the ones who were always looking for Prince Charming and a big wedding. Me, I was happy with just getting an orgasm from a guy—and maybe a little companionship."

"Stop saying shit like that. You deserve the big fairytale as much as anyone else. Everybody's cards are dealt differently in life. The question is how you play your hand to win."

"When did you become Oprah, and I became Stedman?" she joked, and we burst into laughter.

"Baby, you're more like the 'Teen Moms' show," I replied, chuckling, and she fell over, holding her stomach in laughter, tears pooling in her eyes.

For the rest of the evening, we talked, laughed, and looked at old pictures from middle school and college, reminiscing about our younger days.

Chapter Twenty-Three

Angela

A few weeks later, I was standing in the backyard of Granny's house, wearing a light-pink strapless gown. Brent and I had stuck to our plan of just the two of us with the twins and his parents as witnesses at the courthouse. I didn't need a big wedding ceremony like most girls—hell, I didn't even think I would ever get married in the first place.

I watched Jackson and Damon running behind JJ, Tessa, and DJ as they pretended to throw them into the pool. We rarely got together anymore as a family because our lives had sent us in different directions. Emery was working at Brent's company as the vice president and managing her household. Jordan was a teacher part-time and newly married with two kids and one on the way. Plus, she was a stepmom to Damon's daughter. Now, I was married with the kids.

"Little girl, what are you standing over here, daydreaming about?" Granny questioned. She picked up the pitcher of iced tea and poured more into my cup and then hers.

"Old lady, don't start with me. Did the girls give you a hard time today?" I asked, following her to sit on Brent's lap. He wrapped a hand around my waist and kissed me on the cheek and forehead. I sighed in contentment at the peace I felt from having my own family.

"Auntie Angie, can I come over tonight and play dress up with my cousins?" Tessa asked, squeezing between Emery and Jordan on the bench to get close.

"Tonight's not good, baby. I'm too tired from running around and getting the girls settled. Maybe next weekend," I responded, and she looked disappointed. Removing my arm from around Brent, I pulled her on to my lap and grabbed my purse to see what I had that would cheer her up. Normally letting her play in my makeup and nail polish would appease her. Everyone had spoiled her rotten since she was the only girl for a long time.

"How are things at the shop, Angela? I know you had plans of expanding?" Emery asked.

"Things are great for right now. Brent and I set a schedule, so one of us is always home to relieve the nanny at a decent hour. My office manager takes on a lot of the harder tasks. I end up working about three or four days a week for around six or seven hours. Remember when I first started the salon and slept, ate, and fuck—" I said. Brent slapped my thigh, reminding me we had kids around us.

"She's such a heathen. I don't know where I went wrong with raising her," Granny explained and shook her head as everyone laughed at her comment.

"Ain't that the kettle calling the pot black." I chuckled and let Tessa run off to play with the other kids.

"She's right, Granny; you're not so innocent yourself.

Plenty of times, we'd have to call the casino, looking for you when we needed something that Pops couldn't help us with," Emery said, leaning away, so Granny couldn't throw her shoe at her.

"Wait—Granny, you hang out at the casino *that much?*" Damon sassed, walking up on the tail end of our conversation. He bent down and kissed Jordan on the lips, then sat with his arm draped around her shoulder.

"Yep, casino on Saturday night and church on Sunday morning," Granny told us primly, and we all burst into laughter.

"Are you serious? I thought you lived and breathed by the Bible, Granny?" Damon inquired, curiously taking a bite of her famous sweet potato pie off Jordan's plate.

The backyard was decorated with a large, "Congratulations, Brent and Angela!" sign with white balloons and a white dance floor with our initials engraved on it, along with the birthdate of our kids. The deejay's booth sat in the corner, next to the photo booth, and Granny had made all the food, of course. One thing we couldn't get away from was her cooking. Since everything was outdoors, she'd made barbeque, mac and cheese, coleslaw, strawberry sweet tea, and my favorite dessert—chocolate mini-cupcakes—and a wedding cake with our initials on top. Brent wore an off-white tailored suit, and then came home to change into a track suit with our initials and wedding date on the back. I continued wearing my dress.

"I do, and Jesus understands that my little Saturday night is good for the church. What I make the night before, half goes into the collection the next day. I put in way more than those baldheaded bimbos at church," Granny spat, furrowing her brows in annoyance at our teasing.

"Now I see where you get that baldhead term from," Brent commented, and Granny smacked him on the back of the head.

"Shut up, boy, and leave my baby alone."

"Wait, I'm on your side, Granny."

"That woman don't play about me. She can insult me, but don't let anyone else tease me," I said, laughing and passing Brent my glass, so he could take a sip. He held out his right hand and closed it around my palm.

"Can we get back to this Sunday-church thing? So, what do you play, and have you won anything?" Damon asked.

"Damon, my man doesn't have a problem with me, and Jesus doesn't either because He blessed with me a thousand dollars last weekend." Granny smirked and ate another bite of dessert.

Damon shook his head and giggled under his breath. Jordan rubbed his back as his hand rubbed her belly. Everyone knew about the baby now, and Damon wasn't upset with her for keeping it a secret—he was just upset that she'd gotten arrested for helping me. We talked, and we were back on good terms, and I was allowed to keep Tessa again, whenever she wanted to hang out. At first, when Jordan told me he was pissed off at me, I wanted to kick his ass because he would never come between the three of us. Jordan, Emery, and I had a long history and letting some guy tell us who we could see and where we could go wasn't in my definition of being a married woman. But once Jackson pulled some strings and got Jordan's record cleared, our girls' nights resumed.

"Granny, you need to split that thousand dollars with the kids. They could use a little extra in the savings account," I joked, stood and stretched from sitting so long.

"Angela, don't get slapped in front of company for being a smartass," Granny replied, and the entire table laughed.

"Granny, she's a married woman now. You can't be beating on my woman," Brent teased, humorously wrapping a hand around my waist as he stood next to me.

"Guess what, Brent? I was there before you, and I'll be here after you. One thing you can always be sure about is that woman of yours was my responsibility first. Between her, Emery, and Jordan. Well, Jordan was always the good one."

"Here she goes with the Jordan good girl role. On that note, Granny, I love you, but I need to head out and get some sleep," I said, smiling against his shoulder. My skin tingled from his touch on my arm. "You smell wonderful," he said, his breath fanning my skin.

Pops came over, hugged me tightly, and passed me an envelope.

"Pops, I don't need any money. I have my own."

A glimmer of laughter came into his eyes. "Well, save this for my princesses and watch Jazmine's little butt. The other night, she tried to get into everything on the counter," Pops said, leaning down to kiss Marcia on the cheek and rub her feet.

Brent's brow creased. "Yeah, I have to watch both girls, so they don't turn out like their crazy momma. I can see it now—both of them trying to steal a car or jump some boy who ignores the other twin," Brent responded, reaching out to shake his hand.

"Indeed, they will, son," Pops agreed, shaking his hand.

"Congrats again, Angela and Brent. Don't forget the bigger ceremony is still happening next year. Bad enough

Jordan got married in Vegas and left us out, you owe us a big wedding," Emery yelled out and pressed a hand to her mouth to stifle her giggles. I motioned her to hush while the girls slept contentedly in my arms right where they were supposed to be.

Brent grinned at me and opened the back-passenger door, placed Marcia's car seat inside. Then, he came over to me, hovering inches from my face.

"Yes, Brent? Why are you staring at me?"

His voice came as soft as his brown-eyed gaze. "Who am I?"

"Brent," I said, rolled my eyes and blew out a harsh breath.

His arms tightened around me. "Everything is going to be fine; we're officially married now," he said, drawing me into his arms.

"I guess that makes me your wife. Mrs. Angela Townsend."

Brent was laughing deep in his throat, and I leaned up to meet him halfway and captured his mouth.

"How does it feel?" he asked softly as he gazed down into my eyes.

"Honestly?" I said.

"Yeah, Angie." He framed my face between his hands and looked deeply into my eyes.

"I feel no different than when we dated in college. Except now we have two additional people we're responsible for that need our attention. I think we can handle this husband-and-wife lane. Oh, and your nasty ex stays away from us."

"I seem to recall *you* were the one who dated multiple people," Brent said, leaning down to put Jazmine in the car and buckle her seatbelt.

Brent shut the door gently and opened the passenger side. I climbed in and unlocked the driver's side as he walked around to it. Jazmine started to giggle in the back-seat, and I passed her the pacifier from the diaper bag. Brent backed out, his hand on the gear shift as he pulled into traffic.

"We really got married?" I muttered to myself.

We stopped at a red light. Marcia squirmed in her seat. "She sounds just like you," Brent joked, flying through the maze of trees and homes on our block. I leaned over and smacked his chest gently. He gripped my hand and pulled me into a kiss. "Give me a kiss with your spoiled ass," Brent said.

"Whatever, you made me this way. You remember asking me awhile back for a birthday idea spot, and I mentioned Fiji?" I said, pecking his lips.

"You want to go to Fiji for our honeymoon?" Brent questioned, parking in our driveway next to my car. We'd taken his new black Mercedes SUV. I wanted the same one in baby blue as a push gift. He said once I had another baby, I could get one. What he didn't know was I'd bought one for myself already, and it was arriving tomorrow.

"I'm so tired, babe; let's get the girls in bed early. I could use a little alone time with my wife." Brent opened the back-passenger door and passed me the keys to open the front door.

"You're going to milk this whole wife thing, aren't you?" I sassed.

He gripped my ass cheek, held me against his chest, and kissed me deeply. "Yep, so get used to it and go start the bath for the girls. I'll bring them inside."

I dipped my head with a quick nod and walked

toward the house, sliding the key inside. I tossed my purse down on the couch and slid my heels off. Brent walked in with both girls asleep in their car seats.

"Think we should skip the bath and put them straight to bed? They look exhausted."

"That's cool with me. Here, take Jazmine, and I'll get Marcia."

"Oh, and I know about your car getting delivered tomorrow; you're not as slick as you think you are."

"Huh?"

"You call yourself buying your own push gift from Jackson's dealership connection, and you honestly didn't think I'd find out?"

"What did you do, Brent?"

"Ahh, nothing."

"I swear, if you messed with my car, I'm filing for divorce," I spat, picking up a sleeping Jazmine and walking off toward her bedroom.

"Keep telling yourself that. We're stuck together forever, princess."

Chapter Twenty-Four

Brent

You may have thought our first night as husband and wife would be full of long, passionate sex, but after putting the girls to bed, we fell asleep in our clothes.

Today, we both had work, and the girls were getting dropped off at my parents'. Angela lowered herself to the bench and helped feed Marcie, while I fed Jazmine.

"What time is your first client?" I asked.

"Ten thirty. Then, I'm meeting the realtor about more real estate."

"Sounds good. What time are you thinking you'll be free for lunch? I have a surprise for you."

"Brent, you know I hate surprises. Did you buy me a gift like I asked?"

"Even better. Keep your phone on, and I'll call you later to see where you are. Don't be showing off my goodies," I said, kissing her greedily on the lips and opening her mouth with my tongue gaining control.

"Mmm-hmm..."

"Catch you later."

"Okay."

I kissed both my babies, and they tried grabbing ahold of my suit jacket with their sticky hands.

One hour later, I was in the office with Emery, going over the final details of my surprise for Angela. Keeping this secret had been hard but necessary. I'd thrown her off with the car bit and couldn't have cared less about her buying it on her own.

"All righty. Your parents and Granny will watch the kids—and, of course, Jordan and I will help when we can."

"Thanks, Emery. How are things going with you? Jackson said you haven't had any attacks, and your lupus was under control," I said.

"Good. You can say having an amazing husband who's protective and reads up on lupus to be in the know has helped tremendously."

"Nice seeing you back to yourself again, and not letting this beat you down. I remember when you left pregnant without telling Jackson. That fool was ready to hunt you down," I explained shaking my head.

Emery giggled and nodded in understanding. "Don't remind me! Oooh! That man is something else! He reminds me of you and Damon—possessive, protective, and sweet all at once, like a big teddy bear on the inside, but all alpha male on the outside," Emery replied, handing over the pamphlets for the trip to Fiji we planned to leave early on.

"Jackson was telling me you were thinking of cutting back at the office even more

"I want to focus on the kids while they're young. Ever since that Anthony situation and meeting Jackson and having happiness again, I'd opted to really take time while

I can to enjoy being with my family," Emery answered, passing the plane tickets to me.

"Understandable, but Emery, we both know your work brings you happiness. Don't make a quick decision because you're thinking you'll miss out on the kids. Remember, we recently opened the daycare on the top floor. I needed a place for the girls to come when I had them on my scheduled days before Angela and I got back together." I looked at the photo sitting on my desk with all my girls smiling. I felt a protectiveness that I didn't feel back in my younger years. Women often said it was the man who just wanted to date and not make a commitment, but they hadn't met Angela Jones because locking that woman down had taken years.

"How is she doing after that Elena incident?" Emery wondered. Elena went ghost, and I guess that beat down from Angela's cousins did the trick.

"Elena hasn't contacted me or stopped by here, as far as I know," I explained, leaning forward with my fingers laced on the desktop.

"That's good. We don't need Angela getting arrested again; more than likely, it'll be for murder this time. Elena messed with the wrong person. How did you meet her crazy ass anyway?"

"Believe it or not, when we first met, she wasn't like that. She was a confident, funny, headstrong woman who wanted the same things as me."

"So, why did you break up with her?" Emery asked.

"She wasn't Angela," I answered simply and ran a hand over my beard, shaking my head.

"Seems she's in your blood, same as Jackson with me. I can't eat, think, or sleep without thinking about him."

"Once we come back from our honeymoon, what do

you think about having a big celebration party for Granny and Pops? They've given so much to us when they should be retired and vacationing around the world. I know Angela wants to do something." She turned to me, her face lighting up as I spoke about her grandparents.

"Please don't say the word 'retirement' around those two—unless you're ready for an ass-whooping." Emery cackled, heading toward the door, and I followed.

"Think about it, and thanks again, Emery, for getting the trip all set up," I said, bending down to give her a one-shoulder hug.

Feeling my phone vibrate, I took it out and sank back into my chair, seeing a photo Angela sent me of a building she liked.

Angela: *What do you think, husband?*

Me: *What area is this, wifey?*

Angela: *The rich part ;)*

Me: *Are you saying you need an investor?*

Angela: *Possibly. What can I do to get a yes from you?*

Me: *I have a few ideas that include you naked in our bed with your mouth wrapped around something big and long.*

Angela: *See, you can't be saying stuff like that. Now my nipples are leaking, and my pussy is dripping.*

Me: *Come here, so I can take care of that.*

Angela: *I wish, babe, but I need to see the other two locations before I get back to the shop.*

Me: *Damn. Send me a picture once you get back to the salon.*

Angela: *Can you tell me about that surprise?*

Me: *Nice swerve on changing the subject.*

Angela: *What can I say? I learned from the best. Anyway, we'll talk when I get to my destination.*

Me: *Where you now?*

Angela: *Walking into a building to meet a sexy guy.*

Me: *Angela, don't play with me.*

"I like playing games, husband." Angela came inside and locked the door. She walked over and pulled the strings on the blinds, which closed with a loud swoosh. I watched her ass jiggle as she sashayed over to my desk, in the same dress from earlier.

"Surprise," she teased, smiling so hard the corners of her mouth were getting introduced to her ears.

My words fell dead and brittle, like oak leaves in fall. Savoring this moment, I licked my lips and observed her beauty. Even though she was fully dressed, her presence stood bare before me—a new Angela, a new woman who had finally come into her own, rising like a phoenix from the ashes.

"I thought I was the one doing the surprising?" I said, bringing it up to my mouth.

"What's this?" Angela inquired, squinting her eyes at the Fiji pamphlet.

"Since we both kind of did things a little backwards with having kids and eloping, I wanted to give you a honeymoon. I knew Fiji was your ideal place, so I had Emery look into getting us a secluded villa and a private flight. Before you say anything about the girls, Emery arranged for her parents to watch them." I rose to my feet and brought her close to me.

"Aww, baby, you did that for me? Thank you." Angela puckered her lips for a kiss, and I savored them, taking slow pecks. I gripped her thigh with one hand and held her head in place with the other.

"Of course. Now, how about you let me take you out to lunch in your new car?"

"We can drive around anytime; let me give you a little afternoon taste. You're the best friend, husband, and father I could have ever imagined. I think you deserve a little quickie."

"We haven't had an office afternoon delight in a while; I think the last time was when Emery caught us, and you left with your clothes on backwards."

She snorted. "Please don't remind me." Angela held a mischievous look plastered on her face. I leaned forward, giving her another kiss on her lips, running a trail of kisses across her shoulder as she panted and raked a hand down my chest.

The rest of the afternoon was canceled, and she stayed in the office and caught up with Emery, my secretary, and the rest of the office staff, talking about our wedding and showing off pictures of our kids.

Chapter Twenty-Five

Angela

Two *Months Later*

I sat in the doctor's office, getting my annual checkup. The twins were hanging with Emery and Jordan since Brent was working late tonight. Those two munchkins were spoiled rotten. "I can't believe I'm the mother of two kids and married. What has the world come to?" I muttered to myself.

"How's motherhood treating you?" Dr. Lori asked as I placed my feet in the stirrups. Lying on my back, I thought about all the things I needed to do before going to the grocery store and then working on another client's hair later today.

"Let me put it like this, if you want two more kids and a husband to add to your bunch, then I have them waiting for you." I chuckled as she moved around the room, gathering her swabs, gloves, and speculum for my exam.

"Huh," Dr. Lori said as her eyebrows furrowed in confusion.

"What! Is something wrong."

"Calm down, Angela. Let me grab the nurse. I need to do an ultrasound as backup."

"Why?" I panicked and tried to lift my gown up to see what the problem was.

The doctor stepped out of the room, and I tried to get up out of the stirrups, to grab my phone. The doctor walked back inside with the nurse and ultrasound machine.

"Lord, please, if I've done anything wrong in life, I repent. I stole Granny's car when I was seventeen; I lied about sleeping over at a friend's house when I went to LA for Coachella that one summer. Please, let me be okay for my babies." I wiped a tear away as they set up the machine and drizzled cold gel on my stomach.

"Angela, please calm down. I wouldn't want you upsetting the baby."

"Baby?!" I shrieked, ready to pass out at the news of being pregnant again.

Two hours later, I felt like a zombie, walking into Emery's house as the kids ran around the living room. Jordan ran behind DJ and Tessa and almost tripped when she saw me.

"Hey, Angie. What are you doing here?" Jordan questioned.

As I plopped down on the couch, I wiped another tear away and thought about when this could have happened. The strange thing was that I was on birth control because I didn't want any more kids for a while. Possibly never since I wanted to open a second salon.

Jordan came and sat beside me on the couch, waving her hand in front of my face. The kids continued running around and playing games. Soon, Emery walked in holding Jordan's daughter in her arms.

"I thought you had another client tonight, Miss Thing?" Emery asked as she placed the pacifier in Isabella's mouth.

He stared into my eyes intensely with his eyebrows knitted together. I knew he was deep in thought about pleasing me, and then himself. I ran a hand across his bottom lip, tucked between his teeth. Sweat dripped off his forehead, down his nose, and onto my chest. Brent leaned down and gripped my right breast, taking my engorged nipple into his mouth and nibbling gently as he gripped each thigh. He knew I was still a little self-conscious about the baby weight, my breasts getting bigger, and the discoloration—all things they don't tell you to expect during your pregnancy.

"Baby," I forced out. Since the twins' birth, we'd had to settle for scheduled sex dates. I couldn't believe my life had become all about playdates and scheduled sex.

"Tell me what you want," he replied as he leaned up and popped my right breast out of his mouth and captured the left. At no time did his strokes slow up.

A flicker of a smile passed his lips. "Ahh, fuck, you feel so damn good, baby!" He groaned, popping my left breast out of his mouth, and placed kisses up my chest, toward my neck and jawline. The simple things of having his warmth enclosed around me in a protective manner brought more comfort than anyone who'd been in my life.

"Brent... I'm sorry... for..." I stuttered the words out as another orgasm ran from my heels, all the way up toward my core. He leaned up and gently gripped my chin. I bit my lip to stifle the outcry of my orgasm.

"No more."

"No more what?" I asked as his strokes became faster, not letting up to have us come at the same time.

"*Leaving me, baby.* "

"*I won't... ugh! Right there.*"

"That asshole did this on purpose," I mumbled to myself and walked off toward the backroom, as Emery and Jordan were probably watching me, thinking I was losing my mind.

Epilogue

Angela

Chuckling, he pecked my lips, and I wanted to slap him across the face for doing this to me again.

"Brent!" I squirmed with my lips pursed into a pout like a little kid throwing a tantrum.

"Stop fussing before you wake my baby up and stress my son in your stomach," Brent joked. I tried to shove him away as he leaned down and pecked my forehead.

I rolled my eyes, not sure if I could handle a third child, let alone being a new wife and opening a new salon.

"I refuse to give up my dreams, Brent. You know I like to travel and hang with my girls. What about Granny and Pops? They'll be on my ass about staying home and raising your badass kids." I sighed as he lifted my chin to peck my lips, probably thinking it would calm me down.

"You can do all those things, Angela. Stop worrying about stuff that hasn't happened yet. I told you when I proposed, I got your back, baby. Even if I take a little time away from the office, I can have people in place, so I can take care of our kids while you work."

"You'd do that for me?' I questioned in disbelief, running a hand up and down his chest as we stood in the living room while Jazmine wiggled around on the floor with the TV on *Blue's Clues*. Marcia was fast asleep in her playpen.

Brent squeezed me close, leaving little space between our bodies and dipped his nose toward the side of my face. The peace and quiet of just standing together as one gave me peace—even just for a few minutes. "Angela, I won't lie and say kids, work, and marriage will be easy. We can't fool ourselves into thinking life will be perfect. I've loved you since the first time I saw you, babe. Nothing and no one could ever compare. I'll never let you lose yourself in me—or our kids. I fell in love with you because of who you are, not because of who you think I want you to be."

Hearing those words come out of his mouth had me on the brink of tearing up. He wiped the lone tear that attempted to fall and kissed my cheek.

"As long as I have you and our kids, I promise to never let you down." He slowly kissed down my face, connecting his lips to my neck.

"I know you won't. Besides, Granny told me if it came down to it, she'd testify on my behalf, and I would get full custody of the kids if you acted up," Brent joked as my mouth gaped open in shock that she would be on his side.

"That old woman needs to stay out of my business," I whispered under my breath.

"Don't think you're too grown, little girl," Granny spat from the front door, walking inside without calling. Her ears must have been burning.

I shook my head in annoyance. That woman could hear her name from a mile away—even if she were at home. If you talked about her, she'd call you and curse you out. I side-eyed Brent and stepped out of his arms as Granny came inside and shut the door. I went to reach for her coat and purse, and she slapped my hand away.

"Ouch, why did you hit me, old lady?" I asked and rubbed the pain away. Granny pointed at my stomach and then at Brent, shaking her head.

"Didn't I raise you better than that?"

My thoughts went to how she found out I was expecting again before I even knew. Brent bent down and picked Jazmine up, kissing her chunky cheeks and walking out of the living room.

"Don't leave now that she's here. This is your fault I'm in this predicament," I told him with my hands on my hips. My eyebrows narrowed intently on his back as he walked away, whistling a little tune.

"Love you, babe," Brent yelled.

I turned back around and noticed an amused look on her face. I groaned, already hating whatever foolishness she was about to spit out. "Listen, old lady—don't start with me. I'm a married woman, and if my husband wants to showcase his love in all forms, then who am I to stop him?" I explained, crossing my arms.

"I might be old, but I don't hear any complaints from *my* husband," Granny said with a devious grin. She winked at me as she walked into the kitchen, and I followed, helping her out of her jacket.

"You're too old to still be having sex," I muttered and bumped into her as she turned around.

"What was that?" she asked.

"I said thank you for always showing me love and bringing me into your family even when my own so-called mother gave up on me." She nodded and entwined her arm into mine as we walked into the kitchen, watching Brent tickling Jazmine in his arms.

"Have you been in contact with her lately? Your grandfather said she called and wanted to talk with you if you're open to that conversation."

"The mother figure position was filled by you and Pops a long time ago. I don't need anyone else in my life claiming to love me."

Seeing the father and daughter display in front of me showed me I had nothing to worry about when it came to letting go of my fears of falling in love. Having my best friends support me after growing up with a lack of it was all I needed, especially as I took on this new chapter of being a wife and mom.

* * *

Get into a One night stand romance with **Jessica and Joseph**

Heart of Stone Book 3.5 https://payhip.com/b/HGP1

Heart of Stone Book 4 Jessica and Joseph https://books2read.com/u/4NXyPG

If you want more "Mafia Romance, why not try **"Antonio and Sabrina Book 2" Click here** https://books2read.com/u/bpED6g

Have you read *yet* **"Temptation?** That is a stand-alone contemporary, sports, curvy girl romance. Check it out here https://books2read.com/u/mle1Vv

Are you interested in Mafia romance? Check into *Antonio & Sabrina: Struck in Love, Books* 1 https://books2read.com/u/4AxKLo

* * *

Check out **Aydin a grumpy boss, bodyguard romance** here https://books2read.com/u/mBwaOy .Follow my standalone opposites attract, age gap, military romance "**Exposed**" https://books2read.com/u/bQyYZe .

Are you a fan of sports romance? Then download one-night stand, billionaire romance "**Refuel**" https://books2read.com/u/boDyDA. Also, follow it up with workplace, sports romance "**Pressure**" https://books2read.com/u/3Ly1r7 .

If you love romantic comedy, fake relationships, enemies to lovers, find it here, "**Something Gained.**" Click the link https://books2read.com/u/baGLYy .

Any fan of forbidden romance, political? Check out "**Mutual Agreement**" https://books2read.com/u/mgzzWX a steamy romance. Pre-order the full novel of "**Nasir**" here click the link here.

Have you checked out "**She's All I Need**" click here https://books2read.com/u/49lkeW a sports, opposites attract romance. What about dark romance that has everything from steamy romance, opposites attract, suspense, thriller, celebrity, and more "**Joaquin Fuertes Book 1**" https://books2read.com/u/mvZlgV

Catch up with favorite characters in this holiday short romance which includes spoilers. https://books2read.com/u/bzd59G

Playlist

Heart of Stone Book 3 (Angela & Brent)
1. Beyonce Dejavu
2. Chaka Khan Ain't Nobody
3. Jill Scott Crown Royal
4. Anita Baker I Apologize
5. Luther Vandross A House is Not A Home
6. Monica Commitment
7. Normani Waves
8. Pink Please don't leave me
9. No Doubt Don't Speak
10. Rihanna You Da One
11. D'Angelo You're my Lady
12. Rihanna Hard

Reader Questions:

Reader Questions:

1. How many kids does Angela have?

2. What does Angela do for a living?

3. Should Brent have forgiven Angela for breaking his heart?

4. What does Granny always threaten to do if someone makes her mad?

5. Which couple did you like the best?

6. Which husband did you like the best (Jackson, Damon, or Brent)?

7. Who are you more like (Emery, Jordan, or Angela)?

8. What does Jackson do for a living?

9. What secret did Emery keep from her friends and family?

10. What happened to Anthony?

11. Which couple would you like to get a follow up novelette about?

Heart of Stone series

Heart of Stone Book 1 Emery and Jackson
https://books2read.com/u/boWPAV
Heart of Stone Book 1.5
https://payhip.com/b/kWg7
Heart of Stone Book 2 Jordan and Damon
https://books2read.com/u/ba2OMx
Heart of Stone Book 3.5 Bottoms Up
https://payhip.com/b/HGP1
Heart of Stone Book 3 Angela and Brent
https://books2read.com/u/31rx9l
Heart of Stone Book 4 Jessica and Joseph
https://books2read.com/u/4NXyPG

Antonio and Sabrina Series

Order of Reading

The Early Years-A Prequel
https://books2read.com/u/49Zjnw
Ruthless Struck In Love Book 1
https://books2read.com/u/4AxKLo
Savage Struck In Love Book 2
https://books2read.com/u/bpED6g
Beast Struck In Love Book 3
https://books2read.com/u/3LpgdJ
Janice and Carlo Captivated By His Love
https://books2read.com/u/b6je6M
Brutal Struck In Love Book 4
https://books2read.com/u/4NQyE9
Stolen-Fuertes Mafia Cartel Book 1
https://books2read.com/u/mvZlgV
Saved-Fuertes Mafia Cartel Book 2
https://books2read.com/u/4DWwLd
Redemption Struck In Love Book 5
https://books2read.com/u/b5kZ8O

Betrayal- Fuertes Mafia Cartel Book 3
https://books2read.com/u/4A5LGp

Acknowledgments

I want to dedicate this to my team that helps me behind the scenes, from my editors, test readers, graphic designers, and the list goes on. Truly appreciate each of you for keeping me on my toes.

About the Author

Chiquita Dennie is an author of Contemporary, Romantic Suspense, Erotic, Thriller, Mystery, and Women's Fiction. Chiquita lives in Los Angeles, CA. Before she started writing contemporary romance, she worked in the entertainment industry on notable TV shows such as The Dr Phil Show, The Tyra Banks Show, American Idol, and Deal or No Deal. But her favorite job is the one she's now doing full time: writing romance.

A best-selling author and award-winning filmmaker, her first short film Invisible was released in summer 2017 and screened in multiple festivals and won for Best Short Film. Also, she hosts a podcast that showcases the latest in beauty, business, and community called "Moscato and Tea." Her debut release of Antonio and Sabrina Struck In Love has opened a new avenue of writing that she loves.

If you want to know when the next book will come out, please visit her website at http://www.chiquitaden nie.com, where you can sign up to receive an email for her next release.

Catalogue of Releases

Temptation

The Early Years-A Prequel Short Story

Antonio & Sabrina: Struck in Love, Books 1, 2, 3, 4

Janice & Carlo: Captivated by His Love

Heart of Stone, Book 1: Emery & Jackson

Heart of Stone, Book 1.5: Emery & Jackson, A Valentine's Day Short Story

Heart of Stone, Book 2: Jordan & Damon

Heart of Stone, Book 3: Angela & Brent

Heart of Stone, Book 3.5: Jessica & Joseph

Bottoms Up

Joaquin Fuertes (The Fuertes Cartel Book 1)

Cocky Catcher (A Hero Club Novel)

Bossy Billionaire (A Hero Club Novel)

Love Shorts-A Collection of Short Stories

Thank you so much for reading, and if you enjoyed the crazy ride and decide to leave a review, we'd truly appreciate the support.

What's Next

Want to know what happens next?

Follow me on my website to catch the next release.

Reviews are the lifeblood of the publishing world. They're read, appreciated, and needed.

Please consider taking the time to leave a few words on your review platform of choice.

Sign up for updates and sneak peaks at the site below. www.chiquitadennie.com

304 Publishing Company

The home of authors African American, Interracial, Women's Fiction, Fantasy, Erotic, and Contemporary Romance novels. Along with Thriller, Suspense, Poetry, Beauty, and Style Books. Thank you for taking the time out to visit. Join our mailing list to stay updated with new releases and blog posts.

www.ingramcontent.com/pod-product-compliance
Lightning Source LLC
Chambersburg PA
CBHW011201190726
48286CB00009B/2872